Love, Lust, & Infatuation 2

Kandis & Kayla Isaac

Chapter 1: Where Her Only Help is Herself

"The fuck you mean you can't do anything? My daughter was fucking kidnapped from her fucking camp!" I yelled in the officer's face.

"Ma'am, you need to calm down."

"I'm not calming the fuck down until my child is safe in my fucking arms!" I replied, pacing the police station back and forth like a mad woman.

"Baby, calm down," said Kadarius, grabbing me.

"Bitch, don't you dare put your fucking hands on me! Where the fuck were you?! Why weren't you there to get her?!" I screamed, punching him in his chest.

"Look! Yelling at me and everybody isn't going to bring her back, Celly! I need you to get your shit together so we can find out, baby!" he yelled, grabbing my shoulders to keep me from moving. Staring into his eyes, I could do nothing but break down and cry. It seemed as if I'd been crying since I got out of the hospital. I wasn't even supposed to leave the hospital, but after finding out that my daughter was missing, I was ready to go, guns blazing behind her.

Even after explaining everything to the police about Tykell, it felt as if I was talking to a brick wall. I even told them about him calling the hospital and admitting that he took her and I was getting nowhere with them. I felt as if I was going to have a breakdown at any minute. I was stressed that my daughter was missing, I just miscarried with a baby I never knew I had, and I was still baffled that my husband cheated on me with a fucking man. I felt as if I was losing myself, and that was a feeling I haven't had in years.

Kadarius embraced me into a hug, rubbing my back in a

circular motion. After giving my statement to the police and giving them a photo of Cassie for the missing person flyer, Kadarius and I left. Since my sisters and Laurel decided to stay at the police station to talk to the police more, they decided it was time for me to go home and get rest. The car ride was filled with an intense silence. I stared outside the window with tears strolling down my eyes, hoping and praying my daughter was okay.

"We're gonna find her," said Kadarius, breaking the silence.

"What if he hurts her?" I sniffled, looking at him.

"He won't."

"Oh, he won't. Kadarius, do you not remember what the fuck you did to him?! That man is obsessed with me, and he fucking hates you! He has our got damn daughter! He will do anything to try and hurt the both of us. So what makes you think he won't hurt her?!" I yelled. I was so pissed that my lip was trembling.

"When were you going to tell me, huh?"

"Tell you what?!"

"That you were cheating on me with him," he replied, gripping the steering wheel with his nostrils flaring.

"You were fucking a man!"

"And you were fucking a nigga who not only killed your fucking best friend, but he kidnapped our fucking daughter! Don't sit here and try to blame me for everything! Where the fuck were you when she was kidnapped, huh?! Don't try and sit in my face and play fucking victim! You knew what the fuck you were doing just like me! Stop acting as if this is all my fucking fault when it's halfway yours!" he yelled.

"Fuck you! Fuck you, Kadarius! You wanna know where the fuck I was?! He took me from my fucking house and had me chained up to a fucking bed! He almost fucking raped me! I had to fight for my fucking life to get away from him. So, if you were wondering where the hell I was, I was fighting to get away from him! I was in the fucking hospital because I fucking miscarried! Since you're making me out to be the fucking victim, I have every fucking right to be! And you want a real reason to fucking hate me? The baby wasn't yours! As a matter of fact, stop the fucking car!"

"Celly I —."

"Stop the fucking car!"

He slammed on the brakes and I got out, ignoring his calls and yells for me to get in. When he saw that I wasn't budging, he pulled off. I pulled my phone from my pocket and dialed Tykell's number for what seemed like the hundredth time, hoping and praying he would answer.

"Come on, come on, come on, please pick up," I said, hoping and praying he would answer. From the sounds of it, the number was disconnected, and I didn't have any type of way to know what the hell was going on. I found myself at a hotel because I was too paranoid to stay in my home tonight. Every time I received a call, I sent everyone to voicemail. I sat in bed, scrolling through my college yearbook, deciding to do my own research on who the hell and where the hell Tykell was. After doing my research for what seemed like hours, I felt as if I was about to have a heart attack. After finding out what I found out, my anxiety shot sky high knowing that this psychopath had my daughter. My research on him took me back to middle school days. Tykell was on a troubled path since he was in sixth grade, and it showed through all the files I was able to get access to. I felt as if I was running myself ragged all night, trying to figure out at least where his hometown was so I would be able to have a lead on my daughter, but I was going around in yet another circle.

I found myself sitting in my dark hotel room, looking at the city lights outside of my window. It was going on four in the morning, and I couldn't sleep even if I tried. I was stuck in my thoughts, thinking about where I went wrong with Tkell in my past.

"Stop playing, you real talented," said Tykell, passing me my journal back.

"Really?"

"Yeah, really. I don't know why you're so nervous about putting yourself out there. You got the look and the brains, Celly. You got this, and I'm gonna be by your side throughout the entire thing."

"Thanks, Ty. It's just that I always have my doubts."

"Well quit doubting yourself. Everybody here at school loves you, and you're an amazing person. You already have a few selective people who are fans of your work, including me."

"I don't know how many times I can thank you for being here for me."

"You don't have to thank me; you always here for me," he smiled, showing his blue braces. Tykell stood at five foot six, and he was boney and wore glasses. For a college sophomore, he looked like a high school freshman. Tykell was a tech nerd who only hung around a selective few.

"Of course, you're a sweet guy, and your spirit is amazing. I'm so happy we met freshman year."

"I wish other females had that same energy," he laughed, lightly pulling my hand in his.

"Females be iffy when it comes to guys. You just gotta give it time."

"I wish I ran across more females like you. I know you hear me compliment you all the time, but, it's just something about you."

"Something about me, huh? Like what?" I smiled, pushing one of my box braids behind my ear.

"Can I ask you a serious question first?"

"Wassup?"

"What would you do if I told you I lov —"

"Celese, you coming to lunch with us?" asked Kadarius, coming over with a few of his teammates with him.

"Uh, yeah sure. Hey, Ty, we can catch up later? I'm free after lunch."

"I thought you were coming to the rec center with us after lunch," said Kadarius, reminding me.

"Oh yeah. Just text me, Ty. I promise we can talk later."

"It's fine," he replied, looking at me with genuine eyes. As soon as he was about to stand up to hug me, Kadarius pulled me away and *threw his arms over my shoulder, leading me away from him.*

"Why you hang out with him anyway? Something about that lil' nigga don't sit right with me."

"Ty's a good guy. He's my friend."

"Your friend, huh? Well, you need to keep an eye on him."

"Tykell is innocent; I don't need to watch anything. Trust me," I laughed, nudging his shoulder.

Chapter 2: Closet Full of Skeletons

"So, what you gonna do now?" asked my best friend, Lemarcus.

"What the hell can I do?" I sighed, throwing my Bud Light back, taking a long swig.

"I don't know, man. You buried Reggie ass in your ex-wife's backyard."

"Look, this is supposed to be between me and you, my nigga."

"I understand why you did what you did. That nigga took your daughter."

"Yeah," I replied, looking down at my wedding ring on my finger that I never took off. After finding out that it was Tykell's bitch ass who kidnapped Cassie, I felt a wave of regret wash over me for killing Reggie. The image of his eyes rolling to the back of his head was sewed into my brain. The entire time I thought Reggie was behind the crazy antics, and it was an entirely different person. Even though I regret killing him, I felt relieved that I didn't have to put up with his games any longer. If I didn't take his ass out for this reason, I would have taken his ass out for meddling with my life later on in time.

"I at least think you should have put the body somewhere else. When they find out that he's missing, they're gonna go straight to you, especially after that damn email he sent. You're gonna be the first suspect. Man, that's law school 101. You were a married man, you have one of the most successful firms here in New York; you got the perfect life until he airs you out for being a fucking faggot. How do you think this shit is gonna play out, KD? You my boy and I would never knock you for being gay, but how you dealt with the problem was what was fucked up."

"You don't think I know that shit? I never said what I pulled was going to be easy."

"So, what now?"

"I don't know; I might need your help."

"How?"

"Your brother still a cop?"

"Yeah, he's chief of police now. Why?"

"Just keep him on speed dial for me."

"I gotchu, brotha."

"Good."

"Question, though?"

"What's good?"

"Now that Reggie's dead, how are you gonna find Cassie? I know the feds are out here looking for her, but where do you think he hid her?"

"I don't know. But look, I'm gonna hit you later. I gotta go."

"Alright, be safe in that weather," he replied, dapping me up. We parted ways, and I found myself at Celeste's house, standing over the same spot Reggie was buried. I looked down, taking a long pull from my cigarette.

"Damn it, man," I sighed.

I ran my hand down my face, just thinking why shit had to go left. Why Tykell, out of all people, would come back and pull some shit like this. And then it hit me. All the shit I put him through in college answered my question. I just wouldn't have thought he would have come back on a path of vengeance for that. I wanted to kill his ass for touching my wife, for kidnapping my daughter. I wanted Tykell dead, and if someone didn't get to him before I could, I was going to make it happen.

"Let me go!" screamed a terrified Tykell who was being dragged through the woods in only a pair of basketball shorts.

"Nah, not yet," laughed Lemarcus, ignoring his cries in pain from being dragged through sticks and stumps. I watched as my teammates and best friends tied Tykell to a tree before ripping his shorts off, leaving him as naked as the day he came into this world. I approached Tykell as he shivered from the fall breeze piercing his

skin like needles. Taking his glasses, I snapped them in half before tossing them to the side.

"Bitch, I see you hard of hearing," I sighed, flicking him in his forehead.

"What you talking about?"

"You know exactly what I'm talking about, homeboy. Why you following my girl around campus? I thought I told you to leave her alone."

"You don't control what she do and who she hang out with."

"I'm not tryna control her; that's my baby, I would never do that. She can hang with whoever the fuck she wanna hang with, but it becomes a problem whenever I see you gawking at my girl. You follow her around like a lost puppy, and from what I hear, this lil' crush you got on her is getting out of hand — bringing her flowers to each class, buying her lunch every day — shit, you acting like you her nigga. Ain't you?"

"You don't deserve her," he spat.

"Oh, I don't?"

"No, you don't."

"How is that? I think I'm a hell of a man for her. You think you can be better?" I replied, cracking my knuckles.

"Oh, you got no idea," he laughed to himself.

"Enlighten me."

"Well, I would make time for her, unlike you. And I wouldn't cheat on her like you do."

"Oh, I cheat on her? Nigga, where do you see me go to cheat on her? Everybody knows Celeste Braxton is always on my arm. I don't even look at other women. I don't even know why I'm explaining myself to you. That's not what we here for."

"Who said anything about you looking at other women? Just how you claim word going around about me, word getting around about you. I heard you like dick," he laughed.

As soon as that sentence left his mouth, I almost beat his ass to a bloody pulp. My team members had to drag me away before I ended up killing his ass. We spent about a good three hours beating his ass, and after we finished, we left him in the main hall in and out *of consciousness chained to the school's statue for everybody to see the next morning.*

Chapter 3: Motherly Love

Two days later

"Come on, pretty girl. You have to eat," I begged Cassie.

"What part of no don't you understand? I do not take food from strangers."

"If you get to know me, I won't be a stranger."

"Lady, for the last time, I don't want to have anything to do with you. Unless you coming to take me home, stay the hell away from me!"

It'd been a few days since Tykelll brought Cassie home, and it had been pure hell. I mean, I didn't expect it to be easy because after all, he did kidnap her. However, I thought once I showed her some love and affection, things would be better. I understood her being scared of him, but I hadn't done anything to her. This morning, I got up and cooked a huge breakfast. I wasn't sure what she liked, so I made pancakes, waffles, French toast, bacon, eggs, sausage, and grits. I made two plates, took them to Cassie for her to choose, and all she did was yell at me.

Not wanting to feel defeated, I tried again at lunch. Rather than cooking a big meal, I prepared ham and turkey sandwiches. To drink, I brought her some lemonade. Again, she yelled at me and turned me away. This time, I felt defeated. So defeated, that I didn't even bother with dinner. When Tykell asked what I was making, I handed him the leftover sandwiches and stormed off. He knew not to follow me

I went into my room and started to cry. All I ever wanted was to be a mother, but I guess God had other plans. At the age of seventeen, I was diagnosed with uterine cancer. My periods were heavy from the moment they started. My mother took me to doctor after doctor to find out what was wrong. Finally, when I was eighteen, I went to a specialist, and they found the cancer. I was devastated to say the least. Having to have my uterus taken out before I even lost my virginity was heartbreaking. I felt like I was less of a woman and that no man would ever want me. I fell into a deep depression and was even suicidal at one point. That all changed when I met Tykell.

We attended the same college and had a few classes together. I watched him from a distance for a while. I noticed that he was fascinated with this woman in our class. I think her name was Celeste. She had a man, and she clearly didn't want him, but he kept trying anyway. One day after class, I "accidentally" bumped into him. We struck up a conversation and realized we liked a lot of the same things. After talking for about a month, he told me about his mental issues. Being with a man who had schizophrenia and multiple personalities wasn't the ideal situation. However, with me not being able to have kids, I felt like I had to take what I could get.

Since he told me about his conditions, I told him about me not being able to have kids. He didn't want children, so me not being able to have any was a dream come true for him. We got married about six months after we met. For some, that was kind of fast, but I didn't care. I found a man who accepted my flaws.

Everything was perfect for about a year and a half. After that, my urge to be a mother started coming back. With my husband having so many mental issues, adoption was out of the question. I fell back into a depression, and it broke Tykell's heart to see me that way. He came up with the idea to kidnap a child. When he first talked to me about it, I thought he was crazy. However, it didn't seem like such a bad idea the more I thought about it.

Initially, we planned to take a baby from a hospital, but I quickly changed my mind. With the stories of Kamiyah Mobley and Carlina White floating around, I knew that was a bad idea. I wanted a child, but not bad enough to spend twenty years in prison for one. After throwing that idea out of the window, Tykell came up with the idea to kidnap a child. He told me it would require him to be away for a while, and that was fine with me. All I wanted was my child; I didn't care what we had to go to get it.

Chapter 4: The Calm Before the Storm

I sat at the table with my wife, Britney, watching her play around with her food. The first day I brought Cassie here for her, she lit up with excitement. Now that she had Cassie here for a total of four days, I could tell that Cassie was giving her a hard time, which was starting to take a toll on her, I could tell by the way she acted. Britney was bubbly and energetic all the time, but seeing her like this was new to me.

"You good, babe?" I asked, reaching my hand across the table and placing it on top of hers.

"I'm fine, just thinking," she sighed.

"About what? Talk to me."

"She hates me," she replied, running her hands through her hair.

"She'll grow on you."

"It's been four days, and she hasn't come out of that room yet. She only ate one thing out of the four days she's been here. I think she's trying to starve herself. I don't want anything bad to happen to her. If it comes to the point to where she's trying to harm herself, I think we should let her go."

"No."

"Ty, really?"

"Yes. I don't give a fuck if she throw a tantrum and fuck around and kill herself in that room; she's not leaving. You don't know how much it took for me to get her. You wanted a child, I got that for you. Just how I applied pressure to get her, you apply pressure to make her act right," I replied, feeling like she was tapping out on me.

"I understand that but —."

"I don't wanna hear any buts, Britney. Answer me this. You

my wife, right?"

"Yes, Tykell."

"I didn't marry a weak ass woman, and you knew that from day one, that I was always going to be by your side through everything. I need you to be that same strong ass woman I approached on day one."

"I can't with her. You know I can be strong in any other situation, but with this little girl, I can't do it. She's not gonna listen to me. She even fucking cursed at me, Ty. This is harder than you think," she sighed.

"You need a push?"

"What?"

"I said, do you need a push?"

"What type of push?"

"Stay here," I replied, standing up and heading over to the locked room I kept Cassie in. I was growing tired of the agitating games she was playing with my wife. One thing I didn't like was seeing my wife unhappy, and I didn't care if I had to drag Cassie's ass out here kicking and screaming. Approaching the door, I dug into my pocket and fished for the keys. Unlocking the door and pulling it open, I saw Cassie sitting in a corner with her knees tucked to her chest, snot running down her nose, and dry tear stains on her cheeks. It pissed me off seeing her in the same clothes I brought her here in.

Britney was so excited about her arrival that she went out of her way to buy Cassie clothes, toys, and other shit that was far from cheap. Britney even told me that Cassie slapped her while she was trying to get her out of her clothes to take a bath. I approached her, causing her to scurry into the corner further. Chuckling to myself, I knelt down and looked at the fear in her face.

"I see you're giving Brit a hard time."

"Fuck you! Let me go!" she spat.

"Come on now, Lil' Celeste. I know your mama taught you not to use that language," I replied, reaching out to grab her, but she flinched, making me come to a halt.

"I wanna go home."

"This is your home. And you better start acting like it. From now on, you're gonna start addressing that woman out there as your mama, and from now on, I'm your fucking daddy."

"She will never be my mama, and you will never be my daddy," she replied, kicking me, making me catch her leg and grip it hard.

"Listen here and listen good. Your mom cooked dinner for the family tonight. If you don't get out there and wash your ass and eat, me and you are going to have some issues. And you don't want issues with me, Cassie. Now get the fuck up and go wash, so you can eat dinner." I said the last part through gritted teeth, in her face.

"And if I don't?" she edged on.

"I'm gonna beat your ass, like your daddy should have been doing."

"Touch me, and I —."

Before she could finish her sentence, I yanked her up by her arm and dragged her out of the room, kicking and screaming at the top of her lungs. When Britney saw me dragging her out, she stood up with her hand over her mouth.

"Ty, let her go! She's just a kid," said Britney, getting up. But once I gave her that look, she stepped back.

"You didn't wanna handle it, so I told you I would give you a push. Sit down and let me handle it," I said, watching her sit down.

"Let me go!" cried Cassie, trying to pull away, but I yanked her back, ignoring the popping sound of her arm. I threw her in front of me, watching her cry and hold her arm.

"Do we have a fucking understanding yet, Cassie?!"

"I want my mama!" she cried.

Not hearing what I wanted to hear, I took my belt from around my waist and looked down at her.

"Britney, take her clothes off."

"What?"

"Take her fucking clothes off and make her take a bath;

she stinks. I'm not gonna say it again, 'cause if I do it, it's gonna be a problem."

Britney walked over to Cassie with an apologetic look on her face. As soon as she tried to fight Britney, I pushed Britney to the side and ripped her clothes off for her, ignoring her kicks and screams.

"Let her go! That's enough, Tykell!" yelled Britney, rushing over and pulling me off of Cassie. Cassie was now in only her underwear, frightened, and on the floor. As soon as I felt Britney slap me, I grabbed her by her neck, rushing her into the wall, finally snapping.

"Put your fucking hands on me again, and I'm gonna fuck you up. Do you hear me, Brit?" I said, towering over her, tightening my grip.

"Yes," she struggled. I let her go, watching her slide down the wall. I then turned my attention to Cassie and began beating her ass with my belt. One thing I didn't tolerate was disrespect from my woman or my fucking kids. I grew up getting my ass beat day and night, and it never killed me. and by the way Cassie was talking, I could tell she'd never gotten her ass beat. Tossing the belt to the side, I dragged her to the bathroom and slammed the door in her face. When I walked over to Britney, she was holding her neck and shaking her head.

"Did you take your meds today, Ty?"

"No."

"What did I tell you 'bout that? That's why you're acting like this. I've been dealing with this shit for years now, but you know you were wrong. You probably just fucking traumatized that little girl. What the hell is wrong with you?!" she yelled, thinking about what I did to Cassie.

"I told you I was going to give you a push. Make her wash and eat. I'm going out."

"Going where?! You can't keep doing this."

"Doing what, Brit?!" I yelled in her face.

"Not taking your meds, Ty! You know how you get when you don't take them, and that shit isn't healthy! The next time you put your hands on me, I swear to God I will kill you. I love you to death, but one thing I won't do is let you put your hands on me. I used to let that shit slide in the past because I know how much you had trouble trying not to turn into that person you used to be. This person you're becoming isn't the Tykell I fell in love with in college. Get your shit together," she replied, bumping past me and going to the bathroom to check on Cassie.

I stood there looking dumbfounded because she was right. I wasn't myself at all, and I didn't mean to snap the way I did. Shit, I was so frustrated I lashed out when she slapped me because I was already on ten. I never intentionally meant to put my hands on Britney because I loved her. She accepted me for me, and I accepted her for her flaws. Britney was one hell of a woman, even after everything she went through personally. It was as if she was the only one in this world that I had a soft spot for. Instead of rushing into the bathroom to talk to her, I decided to give her her space. I grabbed my keys and decided to go to the bar.

Chapter 5: Time's Supposed to Heal

Celeste

"Come on, Celly, you haven't been home since she's been missing. This hotel looks like shit and so do you. You haven't even changed out of your clothes," said Charlotte, yanking the blinds open, letting the light take over my room like a virus.

"I can't leave," I sniffled, looking down at the missing flyers of Cassie that flooded my bed like a river.

"Yes, you can. Come on, Celeste. Soaking in your own damn stench and staying in here crying all day isn't going to help find her. Come on; I hate seeing you like this."

"I hate feeling like this! I hate this feeling! I just want my baby back," I cried into my pillow.

"And we will get her back. Come on, you can help us hand out flyers today. You need to get out of this hotel," said Laurel, taking a seat next to me and pulling me into her arms.

"I can't d —."

"You can do this, now get up."

"No," I groaned, getting back in bed.

"You know the fuck what? Move Laurel, I got something for her ass," said Charlotte, walking off. I pulled the covers back over my head, not wanting to be bothered. Not bearing to leave this hotel until I got myself right. I was in the dumps for various reasons, Cassie being the main reason. But after being in this hotel by my lonesome, it gave me time to think. It gave me time to think too much, if that makes sense. It was really hitting me hard that I lost a baby, and after miscarrying, the only thing stuck on my mind was, *what if I lost Cassie?* I already lost one child, I couldn't lose another. I was actually depressed and angry at myself for being relieved and happy that Tykell's baby didn't make it. How could I have been so selfish to be happy that my own child died?

In the midst of being under the covers, my body jolted out of the bed when I felt cold water touch my skin. Tossing the cover on the floor, I screamed as the cold water pierced my skin like needles — and the hotel's AC wasn't helping. I jumped out of the wet spot and hugged myself, trying to keep warm, trembling and shaking like a leaf on a tree.

"I can't believe you just did that," I shivered.

"Well, I fucking did. Now, get the fuck up and get dressed. You smell like a pissy ass crackhead and corn chips. You look how Tina looked when Ike beat her ass. Get your ass up and get yourself together."

"Get out, the both of you. I just want to be alone," I groaned.

"I'm not going anywhere," said Charlotte.

"Neither am I," added Laurel.

"Where's Angela? Can't y'all just go bother her?"

"Angela is out there putting out flyers, and we told her we would come and get you. Mama and Daddy are even down here trying to find her. Come on, Celly."

"Charlotte, please get out. I just want to be alone right now," I groaned.

Not knowing what the hell just happened, Charlotte walked up on me and slapped the fire out of me before shoving me so hard into the wall that the picture frame shook. I looked at her with wide eyes, not knowing what the hell I wanted to do or say because I was in shock with how fast she moved.

"Listen here, bitch. Mama didn't raise a punk ass daughter, and she damn sure didn't raise a sorry one either. If you don't get the fuck out of this bed, me and you are going to have some motherfucking problems. Staying in this bed, crying like a got damn hoe who caught an STD ain't helping shit. I understand that you're under a lot of pressure, and so much has happened, but this shit won't break you. I couldn't imagine what the hell that man did to you, and I pray to my God up above that he hasn't done anything to my niece, but this cry baby shit right here gotta stop. You smell like shit, and you look like shit, so take your stank ass in that bathroom and take care of yourself so we can go out here and find my Cassie Pooh. And I don't mean go in there and take no hoe bath, either. Scrub that pussy like Sponge-Bob scrubbed that plate at the Krusty Krab. Don't make me have to rock your shit for real. Please go get ready and come out better than how you lookin'."

I just stood there, looking at her, holding my stinging cheek. I hated to admit it, but she was right. The entire time I had hundreds, probably thousands, of people looking for Cassie, and here I was, stuck in my hotel scared to do anything. I was scared to step foot outside. Bad thoughts of what Tykell could be doing to my daughter clouded my mind like a storm, and I couldn't clear it from my head if I wanted to. It was so bad that I even had nightmares that were so sick, it would make the devil himself cry. I couldn't sleep, I couldn't eat, and I couldn't think without knowing if Cassie was okay. I was such a mess that I didn't even let KJ see me. And I knew how much he missed me, but I couldn't let him see me like this. I knew he was going through it without his twin sister, and he needed to be comforted just like I did.

I looked at Charlotte and nodded my head, agreeing that she was right. Laurel started a bath for me, while Charlotte went to a nearby Old Navy to buy me something simple to wear. I sat in the bathtub, staring off into space, while Laurel washed my back and kept me company.

"What are you thinking about?" she asked.

"What do you think?" I sighed, tucking my knees to my chest.

"She's going to be okay."

"But what if she's not? What if she's not?!"

"Stop thinking like that."

"I can't! I have nightmares every night that my baby is stuck in this fucking cage being treated like a fucking animal, and she's calling out to me, but I can't get to her! I have night-mares that he's going to try and do what he did to me, to her! Tykell almost fucking raped me in that fucking cabin! What if he

—."

"He's not! He wouldn't do that."

"How do you know, huh?! How?!" I yelled in her face.

"God wouldn't let that happen."

"Bullshit. Right now isn't the time for your religious lectures."

"Just how God saved you, God is going to save her. He has angels out there watching her. Just how you got out, so will she. Stop thinking about what if, and think about what's happening now. We will find her, and she will be okay."

I nodded, trying to fight back the tears that were building up at the brim of my eyes. Once I finished taking a bath, I put on the clothes Charlotte bought me. I stared at myself in the mirror, looking down at the yellow sundress that hugged my body and the pair of yellow strap sandals that were on my feet. My hair was pulled back into a nice tight bun, and I decided on a pair of silver hoop earrings with a matching choker.

"Yes, that's what I'm talking about. And just like that, you went from crackhead hoe to let me bend your fine ass over and get a piece. Yes!" exclaimed Charlotte, walking circles around me.

"Shut up. Let's go before I change my mind."

I grabbed my purse, along with the stack of missing person flyers, and followed the woman to the elevator. As soon I pushed the button to go to the first floor, someone stopped the elevator before it could close. A man who stood at about six foot six got on and gave us all friendly smiles before pushing the lobby button. Being the observant person that I am, I admired how chiseled his jawline was, the way the veins on his hands moved slowly, how perfectly aligned his beard was, how sharp his line-up was, and how plump his lips looked. He shared the same complexion as me, and I could tell that he had various tattoos on his chest because his jacket was halfway unzipped.

"Good God, Lord have mercy," mumbled Charlotte, eyeing him up and down.

"Excuse me?" he said, making my jaw drop to the floor. His

voice was like dark, brown velvet.

"She didn't say anything. Hey, can we get a moment of your time? If you don't mind, can you please ask around, and keep an eye out for my niece? She's missing, and we have been trying to find her," said Laurel, passing him a flyer.

"I'm sorry to hear about that. I'll be sure to be on the lookout for her."

"Thank you," I replied, hoping she would return to me soon.

"No problem; you're going to find her."

"I hope so," I sighed.

"Do you mind if I take a few? I can help you pass them out."

"Really? I would appreciate that," I replied, passing him a stack.

"I have a niece; I don't know what I would do if I lost her."

"She's my daughter."

"Your daughter? Damn, I'm so sorry."

"Don't be, just, thank you for helping."

"It's nothing."

Our conversation came to a halt when the elevator doors opened and we all got off. As soon as I was about to walk off, he cleared his throat, catching my attention.

"What's your name?" he asked.

"Celeste."

"I'm Devon."

"Nice meeting you, Devon," I waved, following Charlotte and Laurel out of the hotel.

Chapter 6: Less Than a Man

Kadarius

Due to all the shit that went down, I took a leave of absence from work. There was no way in hell that I would be able to focus with my baby girl missing. There wasn't a minute that went by where I wasn't wondering where she was and how she was doing. Knowing that crazy ass Tykell had her had my mind in overdrive. Ain't no telling what that psychotic fucker was doing to my princess.

Celeste wasn't answering my calls, so KJ had been staying with me. Truth be told, I would rather have them both staying here, but after the way I treated Celeste, I didn't blame her. She doesn't come by, but KJ talks to her almost every day. It's mostly via text, which is fine with him because he hates talking on the phone. Charlotte and Laurel come by often to check on him, and they go out for lunch or dinner together. Surprisingly, he does not seem to be affected much by this. He tells us all the time that his sister is okay and coming home. When we ask him how he knows, he simply says "it's a twin thing". I've always heard that twins can feel when the other is hurt or in trouble, so him saying that gives me some comfort.

Just as Lemarcus warned me, the police came questioning me about Reggie's disappearance. I already had my lawyer on standby, so I went in for questioning without hesitation. Even when my alibi checked out, the lead detective still had me listed as a suspect and began treating it as a murder for hire case. That's when Lemarcus's brother stepped in. He informed the guy that unless they had some solid evidence against me, they had to leave me alone. Once they did, I gave Lemarcus five grand to give to him. To some, that might seem like a small amount to keep the police off my ass, but that was all I could spare at the moment. I didn't know how long I was going to be off work.

I also had planned to pay a private investigator to help find Cassie. When Celeste told me who had our daughter, I did some digging, and the only information I could find on Tykell was shit from college. I even checked under the name Raymon Stevens that he was using and still nothing popped up. It seemed as if his ass disappeared into thin air. There was no telling how many aliases his ass had, so sometimes I wondered if hiring an investigator would do any good. Tears fell from my eyes as I thought about the situation. As a father and husband, I had two important jobs. They were to keep my wife happy and my children safe. I had failed at both. I wasn't the praying type, but since everything happened, I'd been on my knees every night, begging for God to give me a second chance.

"Hey, Dad. You busy?" KJ asked, knocking me out of my thoughts.

He had been so quiet today that I had almost forgotten he was here. We had breakfast together this morning, then he went to his room and I went in mine.

"I'm just sitting here thinking. What's going on, son?"

"I was just checking on you. You look like you've been crying. What's wrong?"

"Just worried about your sister, that's all."

"I figured. Mom is out putting up flyers. I told you guys not to worry. Cassie will be home soon."

"It's not that simple, son. As her parents, it's our job to worry about our children. We are praying she comes home soon."

"She is, Dad! I wish you guys would believe me. She's scared, but not hurt. If she was, I would feel it. I mean, I did share a womb with her for nine months."

I couldn't help but laugh at his statement. I asked him what he wanted me to make for dinner. He told me I didn't have to cook anything because he planned to order us something. Lately, it seemed as if our roles had reversed. He was acting like the parent, while I was acting like the child. We chatted for a little while longer before he went back to his room. When he left, a sense of calmness came over me. For the first time since my daughter had been missing, something told me to listen to KJ.

Chapter 7: Truths Reveal

Three weeks later

Though Cassie had started eating every day, I was starting to give up hope that we would have a mother-daughter relationship. I tried my best to get her to have a conversation with me, but she refused. She simply ate her food and went back to her room. It's only been three weeks, true enough, but I thought for sure I had made her feel comfortable enough to at least talk to me.

Tykell's answer was to beat her and make her talk, but that only made things worse. The longer she was in my home, the more I regretted this situation. After what happened the last time I spoke up, I refused to tell Tykell this. I asked for this, so I needed to deal with it on my own. Tykell was gone for the day, so I decided to sit with Cassie and do her hair. When I walked in the room, she jumped. This was something she had never done before.

"Did I scare you, sweetheart?" I asked her.

"I thought you were him."

"Him? You mean Tykell?"

"Yes."

"No, he's gone for the day. It's just us girls. I'm sorry about what happened a few weeks ago. That was a one-time thing, and it will never happen again."

"He comes in my room at night," Cassie whispered.

"What do you mean?"

What came out of her mouth next threw me off. She told me that when he comes into her room at night, he touches her. My eyes got big as saucers. There was no way in hell that Tykell would do that. Child molesters disgusted me, and he knew that.

In my opinion, they should all be tortured and killed.

"Are you sure you aren't just having bad dreams, sweetie?"

"No, I'm not having bad dreams. He touches me!" she screamed.

I searched for signs of her lying and didn't see any. She had to have been mistaken, though. There was no way in hell this was going on under my roof and I not know about it. Maybe she was mistaken. There had been a couple times where I'd rolled over in the middle of the night, and he wasn't in bed, but that was normal. His mental disorder caused a lot of sleepless nights.

Rather than ask Cassie more questions, I told her to come into the kitchen so I could wash her hair. While I was washing it, all types of thoughts ran through my head. At first, I thought about confronting Tykell, but decided against it. Whether true or not, he would hurt Cassie for saying it. At the same time, I couldn't ignore what she said. Not finding out if it was true or not would eat my conscience up. By the time I had finished shampooing Cassie's hair, I had decided that the best thing for me to do was to see if I could catch him in the act.

Later that night, I went to bed around nine, which was my usual time, and pretended to be asleep. Staying up late at night was something I rarely did, so if I had, Tykell would have known something was up. About an hour and a half later, I felt Tykell get out of bed. I waited about five minutes, slipped out of bed, and tip toed down the hall to Cassie's room. When I got there, I noticed the door was open. I stood in the corner, where I couldn't be seen, but I could see in the room.

Surely there's no way he's touching her if he has the door open, I thought to myself. Boy, was I wrong. Tykell was sitting on the bed beside Cassie caressing her thighs with one hand and her chest with the other. Vomit rose from my stomach to my throat. It took everything in me not to puke my guts out. I couldn't believe what I was seeing. Accepting Tykell's mental disorder was one thing, but there was no way in hell I was staying with a child molester.

"Please stop," I heard Cassie cry.

"Shut up. If you don't stop crying, I'll make it worse."

"I want my mommy."

"You won't be seeing Celeste ever again."

When I heard Celeste's name, my blood started boiling. I knew Cassie looked like somebody I knew, but Celeste was the last person I would have thought of. I thought Tykell's obsession with her stopped after she made it clear that she didn't want him. She'd even gotten married I heard. He was supposed to kidnap a random child, not the woman he was obsessed with. Rage filled me as I realized that taking Cassie had nothing to do with me. It was about Tykell. I went back to my bedroom in anger. Tykell was going to pay for this shit.

"Yes, dear?" he asked when he came back in the room.

"I have a terrible headache, and I'm out of aspirin. Could you run to the gas station and get me something?"

"Of course, baby. I'll be right back," he said as he grabbed his keys and wallet from the dresser.

When he was out of the door, I got up and went to Cassie's room to check on her. The gas station wasn't far, but whenever Tykell went, he talked to the cashier for a while. When I got in Cassie's room, she was laying on the bed crying.

"He touched me again."

"I know, sweetheart and I'm sorry. I promise it won't happen again. Listen, I need you to do something for me. There is going to be some yelling coming out of my room. No matter how loud it gets, stay in your room. Oh, put some clothes on too. Once everything is done, we are getting the hell out of here."

"Can I go home?"

"Yes, sweetheart, you can go home. Now do as I say."

I kissed her on the forehead and went to the garage to get the tools I needed. After that, I rushed back into the bedroom just before I heard Tykell pull up. He walked back in the bedroom and tried to hand me a bag. I took one of my hands from behind my back and took it.

"I got you a Pepsi too, babe. Why are you out of bed?"

"I heard Cassie crying and went to check on her."

He had a look of fear in his eyes after that.

"What did she say was wrong?"

"Don't play dumb with me, Tykell. You know exactly what's wrong with her. How could you?"

"Look, I don't know what that little bitch told you, but she's lying."

"I saw you, you sick motherfucker! Oh, and just when were you going to tell me she is Celeste's daughter?"

He stood there silent.

"Oh, now you on mute?"

"I can explain."

"Explain it to Satan when you get to hell."

Before he could ask what I meant, I swung the hammer I had behind my back and bashed him in the head. He yelled as he stumbled, and I hit his ass again. This time, he hit the floor. I stood over him with the hammer, bashing his head over and over. His blood was everywhere, but I didn't care. His ass deserved this shit.

Once I was done with the hammer, I went back to the garage and got the saw that I had laid out, then went back in the room. I took the saw and began slicing off the hand that he used to touch Cassie. After I got it off, I got up to go grab my stuff so Cassie and I could leave. I packed a few clothes and some money I had stashed away for a rainy day. It was about three thousand dollars. In my secret bank account, I had about five thousand. Even though Tykell took care of me, I wasn't stupid. My mother always told me to have some mad money stashed. That was the perfect name for it, because I was mad as hell right now.

When I was done packing, I started walking out of the room. Before I got all the way out, I stopped and looked around. This was the last time I would be in here. I looked down at Tykell's body and for some reason, I had a flashback of me watching him touch Cassie. I put my bags down, got the saw, and went over to Tykell's body. After pulling down his pants, I sliced his dick off. He may not have raped her, but something told me he would have if I hadn't have found out. Once his dick was off, I placed it in his mouth and walked out.

Chapter 8: Faith and Reassurance

"Come on, you're really telling me you haven't gotten any news on my daughter yet?" I stressed to the detective who has been following the case since day one.

"Mrs. Norwood —."

"It's Ms. Braxton now. Fuck all the formalities, Detective Gates. It's been a month damn near and you're telling me you still haven't found my baby."

"We are trying the best we can."

"By sitting on y'all ass!"

"Look, Mrs. Norwo —, I mean Ms. Braxton, we are doing everything in our power to bring Cassie back home to you. I know you're worried about her, but you have to let us do our jobs."

"Right. Let y'all do y'all jobs," I scoffed, shaking my head.

"I promise, I will let you know if I even hear a whisper about Cassie."

"I hope so. Me and my ex-husband are up here day in and day out trying to find out where she is. And I just feel as if you all could be doing more."

"I'm sorry to inform you, Ms. Braxton, but you are up here more than Mr. Norwood. Your ex-husband has only been up here three times this month."

"Really?" I said in disbelief.

"Yes. But I am indeed a very busy man. I will give you a call, Ms. Braxton." he replied, basically pushing me out of his office. Running my hands through my hair, I walked out of the police station, headed to my car. Looking over at the missing person papers in the passenger seat, I picked one up and fought back the tears, trying to keep the thought of my baby being dead out of my head.

"I'm going to find you, baby girl," I sniffled, talking to the poster.

Putting it down, I drove to my new apartment on the Upper East Side. After somewhat getting out of the funk caused by Cassie being missing, I decided to finally go back home. The first night I spent in my house alone was dreadful, and I hated it. It felt as if everything from that night replayed in my head as soon as I stepped foot back into that house. I had a nightmare so realistic that I felt like I couldn't wake up from it. I still owned my home, I mean, I would never sell the first piece of property I ever purchased after my career kicked off. I just needed a temporary place to stay until I could get right with myself well enough for me to move back in.

Parking my car, I got out and went inside. As soon as I sat down to get comfortable, my phone began to ring. Thinking it had something to do with Cassie, I damn near broke my neck trying to get my purse. Dumping everything out and watching it hit the floor, I quickly grabbed my phone and answered, pressing it to my ears.

"Hello, hello," I answered frantically.

"You gotta calm down when answering the phone," said Devon, making me sigh and roll my eyes.

"I thought you were one of the detectives calling about my daughter."

"My bad, how's the search going?"

"Apparently not good."

"You're going to find her."

"I wish everybody would stop telling me that. It's like people are just saying it to say it now."

"I'm saying it because I have faith that you will."

"I know."

"Then act like you know; you got this, Celeste."

"Thanks, Devon." I smiled weakly.

"No problem."

"No, seriously. Thanks for everything."

"How you mean?"

"Thanks for helping me look for her and keeping my spirits up. I would have never thought you would have come back to me for more flyers to help me look."

"I don't like seeing a mother in distress."

"Well, that's good to know." I laughed lightly to myself.

"Yeah."

"So, what did you call for?"

"To check on you, pretty much. I haven't heard from you in a minute. You would usually text me, and I thought you were ghosting me for a second."

"No, I wouldn't ghost you unless I have a reason."

"Hm."

Beep, beep, beep, beep

"Hey, can you give me just a minute to call you right back? I have another call coming through."

"Yeah, go ahead. I have to get to work in the next hour. Just hit me tonight."

"Okay, bye."

"Bye, beautiful."

I clicked over without looking at the caller I.D. I had to get out of the habit of being so eager when answering the phone, but I knew I couldn't. It was as if every time my phone rang or dinged, I had to answer it swiftly.

"Hello," I answered.

"Is this Celeste Norwood?" asked the woman on the other end.

"This is she. To whom am I speaking to?" I replied, not even bothering to correct her, in case it had something to do with Cassie.

"You have a package waiting at your home. Can you please come as soon as possible to pick it up?"

"A package? Wait, I didn't order anything."

They didn't even say anything. They just hung up, leaving me dumbfounded. Not being able to rock my Christian Louboutin's how I usually do, I kicked them off and put on a simple pair of white Nike slides. Grabbing my laptop, I just sat there, staring off into space, not even able to write. After going to therapy, my therapist suggested that I write out my experience to try to cope with what happened to me. It seemed as if the more time I had to myself with my laptop, the more I couldn't find it in me to relive that moment. I understood the reasons, but I just couldn't. Stripping out of my sundress, leaving me in nothing but my white lace thong and matching lace bra, I walked to my bedroom and simply changed into a pair of Nike sweatpants and a regular Nike tank top. Hearing knocking at my front door, I approached it and looked through the peephole to see Kadarius. When I opened the door fully, I saw that he had KJ with him.

"Hey, Mommy!" yelled KJ in excitement, running up to me and hugging my legs.

"Hey baby, Mama missed you so much." I smiled, kneeling down to his level and kissing him all over his face.

"I missed you too."

"Good, now go put your things down. I'll be there in a minute. Let me talk to your daddy real quick."

I watched as he ran inside, and I blocked Kadarius from coming in. That was something he always tried to do since I moved, come inside. He knew the both of us were only cordial for the moment, and every time we were around one another, he tried to push his limits. He still had this idea in his head that we were going to get back together, but he knew good and well that it wasn't going to happen.

"So, you haven't been to the station I hear," I stated.

"I called."

"Wow, like a call is going to do something."

"Don't start this."

"Don't start what? Kadarius, I never would have thought that you would have given up."

"I'm not giving up on her."

"Then what the fuck do you call it? I feel like I'm the one out of all of us who's the most fucking worried."

"Are you questioning my feelings for my daughter?"

"Yes, I am questioning them. You only fucking cried one week out of the whole month and some change she's been missing. Me? I've been losing sleep, weight, I even lost fucking hair looking for her, Kadarius. It seems as if you stopped caring."

"I would never stop caring about her! Don't ever do tha —."

"Fuck you. Get away from my door."

"Celly, we really doing this? I don't feel like arguing with you."

"Goodbye, Kadarius," I replied, shutting the door in his face. I shook my head, turning around to KJ, who was playing on his Nintendo Switch.

"KJ, baby, do you wanna come with me to go pick up a package from the old house?" I asked him. I didn't want to keep him in this house like a prisoner just because his sister was missing. It was as if KJ was stapled, glued, and duct taped to my hip every time we were together. My eyes never left off him, no matter what. I felt as if I was suffocating him sometimes, but I didn't care. Whenever he came over with me, I would never take him outside or anything.

"Yeah," he smiled.

"Okay, baby."

"Oh, Mommy, can we eat pizza?"

"Of course, baby, come on," I smiled.

I grabbed my keys and wallet, which were still on the floor from earlier. KJ and I went down to my car. Once I buckled him inside, I got into the driver's seat and put my key into the ignition. Cranking up, I pulled out and made my way to my other house. Hearing my phone ring once more, I sighed picking it up.

"Yes?" I asked, not even knowing who it was.

"Yes, I called earlier."

"About the package?"

"Yes."

"I'm on my way now."

"Great. Do you have me on speaker?"

"Uh, no and why does it matter? Who are you?"

"Don't worry about who I am; just know I know who you

are."

"Excuse me?"

"Just know I'm bringing you something that you've been looking for, for a while now. I don't want you to say anything because I don't want to hear anything you have to say. Just know that I know you and we both have something in common. We both are victims of a man who fooled us in the beginning. The thing is, you got away in a short period of time, and it's taken me years to get away, to find out the monster that man really is. I know how it feels to lose something, to not have something so bad that you would do anything just to have it. Then I realized taking something from someone else is gonna do nothing but hurt that person more than it hurt me. Just know when you arrive at your place, I'm gonna be long gone. I knew he loved you more than he loved me. I thought it was just a simple, stupid college crush, but I would have never known his infatuation with you would have gotten to this point. Look, what kept me going knowing that I couldn't have children was faith and reassurance, and my faith and reassurance will forever be with me no matter what. Shit, I know that's all you're hanging on to right now."

There was a short pause on her end while I pulled into my yard. When my eyes met Cassie sitting on the front porch with a cover on her shoulders, my spirit almost left my body.

"Just know, I got rid of him for her, you, and me. Goodbye, Celeste," she said before hanging up. I almost kicked the door off the hinges trying to get out of my car. When Cassie saw me, she ran into my arms, crying. We sat there, shedding tears together. I dropped to my knees and pulled her into my arms.

"Oh my God! Oh my God! Cassie, I missed you so much," I weeped, holding her so tight, I could take her breath. She was so emotional; she couldn't even speak. I heard KJ get out of the car, and he couldn't help but to cry. He jumped into my arms as well before hugging onto Cassie.

Chapter 9: In the Blue

Devon

"Come on, Ma. Today is about you. Why every time I take you out, you have to make the topic about me?" I sighed, looking over at her and my other siblings. Her birthday was in two days, so my siblings and I decided to take her out early to celebrate. We knew our father wouldn't let us steal her away on her special day because every year, he had this huge birthday week trip planned for her. My siblings and I rented out the best rooftop restaurant in New York for the afternoon, and it was beautiful out here. But no matter how beautiful the view was, I knew my mother wasn't going to sit this lunch out peacefully without pecking at me. My mother and my siblings would always clown me about not having a woman on my arm when we got together — it never failed. All of my siblings were either married or in a relationship. And some even had kids, except for me and my older brother, Sebron.

My big sister, Jozlyn, was married to her high school sweetheart for eight years, and they had five kids, working on number six. My little sister, Gabby, just finished her senior year at Spelman and was now engaged to her college boyfriend, who attended Morehouse. Shit, even my seventeen-year-old twin brother and sister, Harvey and Hope, had boyfriends and girlfriends. Every time we got together, my mother tried to ship Sebron and I off to every woman she saw fit for us.

"I know, but do you know what would be the best present you could give me?" she smiled, placing her hand on top of mine.

"And what is that?" I smiled, already knowing the dumb response I was going to get from her.

"To go out and get a woman."

"Oh lord, here she go," laughed Jozlyn.

"What? I just don't want my baby to be alone his entire

life," she playfully pouted, before taking a sip of her Moet.

"I'm not gonna be alone, mama. I'm only twenty-six."

"And going on thirty," she scoffed.

"I don't know why you even bother with her; you know she's not gonna stop until we bring a woman home to her," laughed Sebron, fixing the collar on his red and white Tommy Hilfiger Polo he sported with the matching pants.

"See, your brother know."

"Mhm, right. Enough about the love life I don't have," I smiled, showcasing my nice set of teeth.

"Right, so how's work going?" asked Gabby.

"Work is work."

"Oh, really? come on now, stop lying. You're the best photographer and director in New York. I know it's not just "work is work," she replied, mocking my tone.

"Work is work aight. I took a few photos of a few celebrities last week."

"Ohh, how does it feel to be around a celebrity Devvy? I'm still mad you took Beyonce's photos and didn't set up a meeting for me to meet her. You know she's my idol. Ohh, have you met Roddy Ricch yet? Oh my God, that man is so fine," said Hope, badgering me with questions back to back.

"No, I haven't met him yet. Can you calm down?" I laughed at her excitement.

"I am calm."

"Don't look like it. Talking about some Robby Itch. Girl, you better be focusing on them books and not them lil' rappers you love so much."

"Mama, his name is Roddy Ricch; put some respect on his name, please," she scoffed.

I laughed watching them bicker back and forth about the little things. Times like this made me miss the old days living back in Chicago. Even though the violence and the tough streets of the Chi made our childhood difficult, we learned a lot from the struggles we'd been through. My mom and pops broke their back day in and day out to get us through school and to get us out the hood. My dad worked three jobs while my mom worked two. What stopped me from getting into a relationship was knowing that I wouldn't be able to find a female out there who wanted what I wanted. I wanted the same love my parents had — the loyalty, the bond, the love. The loyalty, the bond, and the love they had. They literally took turns taking care of us while the other worked on getting their degree. My mother was an orthopedic surgeon, and she recently just received her license to do plastic surgery, while my father was the chief of police.

I was about to dig clean into my T-bone steak until my phone started ringing next to my plate. I held my finger up for everyone to excuse me, before getting up and stepping away. A small smile spread across my face upon seeing Celeste's name flash across my screen.

"Hey, how's it going?" I asked.

"You know you're an angel, right?"

"Thanks for the compliment, but why, though?" I asked, looking confused as if she could see me.

"I found my daughter."

"That's amazing; I'm happy for you. Is she okay?"

"She's a little shaken up. We're at the hospital right now examining her. She hasn't done much talking since we found her, but she's here. I just wanted to call and thank you."

"There's nothing to thank me for."

"Yes, there is. You kept my head held high when I couldn't. When I had doubts, you talked me out of it and you helped me a lot. I just wanted to call and tell you because I wouldn't feel right not doing so. If it wasn't for you, my sisters, and my parents, I don't know if I could have made it this far.

"You're strong, beautiful, and smart. Trust me, I knew you would have made it."

"Here you go with the compliments."

"You gave me one; wouldn't be right if I didn't return the favor."

"You're right." I smiled hearing her light laugh over the other end of the phone. There was something about the way a woman laughed.

"I know I am."

"Well look, I gotta go. Thank you again."

"You're welcome, beautiful."

"Bye, Devon."

"Bye, Celeste."

Hanging up the phone, I turned around to the table to see it as quiet as space. All I could do was sigh because I knew they were ear hustling. Walking back over to my seat, I began cutting into my steak, ignoring all eyes on me.

"When did you start walking away from us to take phone calls?" asked my mother with a raised eyebrow.

"Who's Celeste?" asked Gabby.

"Dang, I thought that phone call was for me." I laughed.

"Tell her we wanna meet her," said Hope, before shoving a spoonful of garlic mashed potatoes in her mouth.

"Stay out of my business, dang."

After eating with my family, taking photos, and taking my mother shopping, I found myself in my apartment, standing over at my window, looking over at the busy New York streets. I just finished taking a shower, and instead of getting fully dressed, I only wore my gold and black silk Versace robe. Walking over to my office, I sat down and opened my drawer, pulling out my memory card from one of the recordings I took three days ago. Popping it into my laptop, I opened the file and looked at my work. After editing it, I emailed the final copy to my customer, who I knew would be satisfied. All I could do was stare back in awe at the masterpiece I was watching. I was the director of King's Playhouse. King's Playhouse was damn near the biggest porno company in the world. If they got any bigger, they would be giving Playboy a run for their money.

They had the baddest pornstars known to man. They also had the kinkest shit that would make the devil look away. This was one part of my life I always liked to keep private, but if it got out, I wouldn't mind. The only thing that kept me from letting the world know about my secret job was the respect I had for my parents. Yeah, I took pictures and directed music videos for celebrities all over, but directing pornography was something different, something that intrigued me.

Sadly, being behind the camera wasn't something I truly wanted to do anymore. I wanted to be in front of the camera; I wanted to be in the spotlight. But I knew I couldn't and I wouldn't. Shit, I was one freaky ass nigga. I think being too freaky was what ended my last relationship to be honest. I was the type of nigga to eat your soul out while we eat thanksgiving at your grandmother house. I was the type of motherfucker who would send you a video of me busting a nut while you're in church.

I was more so single by choice, but every time I explained that to my family, they called bullshit. They rarely knew things I did behind closed doors, and that was the issue. The issue was that I knew I wouldn't be able to find a woman who would accept me for who I really am. Shit, I was a good ass man, not to sound cocky or anything. I'd treat you right, be loyal, and fuck you like a real man is supposed to. I'd make your dreams come true if I could. I had more money than I could count, so spending half a mill on you was chump change to me. Baby, if you wanted your own business, I would buy the building right now and support whatever you were selling. My girl could be selling her nudes, and I would still support her if that was something she truly wanted to do. I grew up in a supportive household, so one thing I wasn't afraid to do is support you.

Pausing the video on my Macbook, I pulled my cell phone from my robe pockets and dialed Serenity's number. Serenity was my childhood best friend, my first girlfriend, my first nut, and she was currently my fling when I needed to release some tension. Serenity was on the thick side — I loved a thick woman. If you weighed two hundred pounds and a lil' over, you were my type of woman. The way Serenity looked made me go for BBW's. She had legs like a stallion, her perfect DD breasts set up as nice as an old school Cadillac, her stretch marks resembled cinnamon rolls, and her toffee-colored skin was as smooth as caramel. Her stomach used to hang over, and I wasn't even gonna lie and say I didn't liked that shit; I was a sucker for natural women. I guess she didn't, because in the end, she got lipo.

Serenity was the number one pornstar of King's Playhouse. She was technically the Beyoncé of the porno industry. She even had paparazzi follow her around sometimes. The shit we did together would make a nun lose her religion. When I heard her sweet voice over the phone, I smiled, tracing my tongue across my lips.

"Hey."

"Wassup," I smiled, with my voice deep and raspy. I looked over at the clock on my wall that read three thirty in the morning.

"I was gonna ask you the same thing."

"You know what I want. You already know what be up when it's three in the morning."

"Oh, I know. I was gonna call you myself. Thinking about what we did last week got me dripping like a leaking faucet."

"How wet is it?" I asked, before hitting the FaceTime button. As soon as she answered, my soldier stood at attention, seeing her fully naked, watching her play with her fully erect nipples. She lowered the camera to her pussy, and I bit my lip, feeling the pulse in my dick jump. Untying my robe, I placed my dick in my hands, stroked it, and watched her juices glisten her second set of lips like diamonds.

"Get dressed and come over before you give a nigga a heart attack."

"How you gonna have a heart attack?"

"Got my heart racing fast and shit. Bring your ass over here," I chuckled lightly.

"I'm coming, Daddy," she smirked, pulling the camera to her face and licking her juices from her fingers like candy.

"I'll see you when you get here."

"One more thing."

"Wassup?"

"How much you love me?" she asked.

"You know I love you to the moon and back, Ren," I smirked, calling her by her nickname.

"Well, do that little thing with your tongue that I love so much."

"I got something better than that, wear my favorite color."

"Blue it is."

Chapter 10: Getting Back to Normal

"So, you mean to tell me, you got a phone call telling you to go to the house, and Cassie was just sitting there?" I whispered to Celeste as the doctors looked over my baby girl.

When KJ called and told me they had Cassie, I was beyond happy. God had finally answered my prayers. Despite how Celeste thought I should be reacting, I was worried sick about my child. Though I was glad to have her back, the circumstances of how she came back were a little shady to me.

"That's exactly what happened. Why do you ask?"

"Just sounds a little strange, that's all."

"It is strange, but we got our daughter back. That's all that matters."

"Yeah, I guess you're right."

"You guess?"

I was about to say something when the nurse came out.

"Mr. and Mrs. Norwood, she's asking for you both."

When I got there, Celeste told me they were performing a rape kit on Cassie. I hoped like hell that bitch nigga hadn't touched her. I had already bodied one nigga, doing another one would be easy.

"Daddy!" Cassie yelled as she jumped into my arms.

"Baby girl, I missed you so much. Are you okay? Did they hurt you?"

She dropped her head, letting me know that something traumatic had happened to her.

"The doctor would like to speak with you guys in private. I can stay in here with Cassie."

Cassie looked like she wanted to protest but agreed once Celeste asked the nurse if KJ could come in also. When he came in, Cassie fell into his arms. Watching them embrace almost brought tears to my eyes. After making sure the twins were good, Celeste and I went in to speak with the doctor.

"Mr. and Mrs. Norwood, please have a seat," the doctor said.

I sat down and prepared myself for the worst.

"We did a rape kit on Cassie and we did not find any bruising or signs of sexual assualt."

"Thank God!" Celeste shouted.

"She did, however, inform me that she was molested."

Rage filled my body as I thought about that nigga's hands on my daughter. Once again, I felt like I had failed as a father.

"She isn't malnourished or dehydrated. Other than the molestation, it looks as if she was cared for. You can take her home now."

"Thank you, doctor," Celeste and I said in unison.

After getting Cassie's discharge papers, we left. The kids rode with Celeste, and I followed them to her house. Once we got inside, Celeste took Cassie upstairs to help her get a bath while I sat with KJ.

"Told you she was coming home, Dad," he told me.

"You did! I'm glad she's back. Did she tell you anything?"

"She said the lady she was with kept trying to force her to call her Mommy. When she wouldn't, the lady got sad. The man who took her touched her between her legs and on her bum bum. She told the lady about it. The next time he did it, the lady told her it wouldn't happen again."

I wasn't sure who this woman was, but I was starting to thank God for her. It seemed as if she took good care of my daughter. After Cassie's bath, she came to the living room and laid in my arms.

"I missed you, Daddy."

"I missed you too, Princess. Do you want to stay here with Mommy or go home with me?"

"Why can't we all stay together?"

I wasn't sure how to explain to her that Celeste and I

weren't together anymore. I looked to Celeste, and she was just as stumped as I was.

"Sweetie, Mommy and Daddy aren't seeing eye to eye right now, so we are living separately. You and your brother will spend some days here and some days at his place."

In my opinion, this wasn't the best time to explain our separation for her but speaking up would surely cause an argument between me and Celeste.

"Can we all stay together for a few days? At least until Cassie gets used to being home," KJ asked.

Leave it to my son to come up with a solution to our mess. I looked over at Celeste, and I could tell she was thinking about the best way to turn down KJ's offer. However, much to my surprise, she agreed.

"Daddy can stay in the guest room. Just for a few days, though."

"Thank you, Mommy!" Cassie screamed.

Celeste cooked dinner while the twins and I watched TV. Once it was done, we all sat down and ate like a family. Even though I hated the reason we were together, it felt good having my family back. The kids seemed to be enjoying it as well. It was then that I decided that no matter what I had to do, I was going to get them back. First, I needed to find out more about this mystery woman.

The evil person inside of me was saying that maybe Celeste set this kidnapping up to get my attention. The angel in me knew that she would never do anything like that. Still, I needed confirmation. After the twins went to sleep, I went to the living room to talk to Celeste.

"Call her," I said.

"Call who?"

"The woman who brought Cassie back. I'm sure you still have the number."

She pulled out her phone and did what I asked.

"Is everything okay?" the mystery woman asked when she answered.

"Yes, everything is fine. My husband and I were calling to thank you for bringing our daughter back."

"No need to thank me. It was the right thing to do. I'm sorry for causing so much pain. I wanted a child so bad that I would've done anything to get one. I thought the man I loved took Cassie for me, but it was to spite you. I not only found out that she was your daughter, but I also found out that he was a monster. Killing him won't change what happened, but it will bring both of us peace. It will be hard, but I have to pick up the pieces of my life and move forward. I'll call back in a few days to check on Cassie, if you don't mind."

I told her it was and thanked her before Celeste hung up the phone.

"Britney," Celeste said.

"Britney?"

"There was a woman who was fascinated with Tykell in college. I'm almost sure that's who the woman is."

I had no idea who Britney was, but I thanked God for her.

Chapter 11: Sparks Fly

Celeste

Four Months Later

"How do I look?" I asked Charlotte, twirling around, showcasing my outfit. I was finally going on a date after four months. Charlotte and Angela decided to come over and help me decide on what to wear. It took a lot for me to actually agree to go on a date after everything that happened with Tykell. If a man looked at me in any way, I was scared, thinking he would do something to me. It took monthly therapy sessions and a lot of praying for me to actually agree to stepping out there again. What makes matters worse was that everyone knew who I was due to me being on the news when Cassie went missing. I knew I said I wanted more exposure for my work, but that was the wrong type of exposure. I haven't touched the keys on my laptop since this whole situation. Shit, I haven't been myself since the entire situation.

"Bitch, you look fuckable. Yasss!" yelled Charlotte, coming over and walking around me.

I plainly wore an all-white, one long sleeve, off the shoulder, asymmetrical dress with a pair of Dolce & Gabbana patent leather sandals with logo heels. I looked down at my freshly painted cream-colored toes before turning around to face my sisters.

"You look amazing," said Angela, getting up and approaching me, fluffing out my loose curls.

"Thank you. Are you still taking Cassie and KJ with you to Vermont?"

"She didn't tell you?

"Tell me what?"

"She doesn't wanna go. She said she wants to stay with you. Is everything getting better with her?"

"Sadly, no, things aren't getting better." I sighed, taking a seat in front of my vanity.

"Therapy isn't helping?" asked Charlotte.

"At first, we thought she was getting better, but she's not. She had nightmares for two months straight, she's depressed, and she's starting to not talk to us again. I'm not even gonna lie and say I'm not worried, because I am. I thought she was getting back to her old self, but she's not."

"I'm sorry that shit happened to her. Lord knows what else he did to her."

"The doctors did a rape kit; they said he didn —."

"You can't trust that shit sometimes. Did she tell you everything that happened?"

"No, the only person she talks to is KJ."

"What did KJ say?"

"That she told him that Tykell came in and touched her every night."

"That sick bastard is gonna rot in hell. I hope somebody off his ass," said Charlotte.

"Someone already did."

"How do you know?"

"Just know that I know," I replied, keeping the conversation Britney and I had to a bare minimum.

After everything happened, Britney called every day to check on Cassie, and sometimes I answered, sometimes I didn't. In the beginning, I just answered her calls because I was grateful that she brought my daughter back to me, but then it dawns on me that she was the reason Cassie was taken in the first place. I felt bad that she couldn't have kids, but that didn't give her a right to have mine taken from me. I knew it wasn't only her fault, but my daughter was emotionally traumatized, and I feared that if she got older and still carried this with her that she would do something horrible.

"Look, I gotta go. Please keep an eye out on my baby," I said, grabbing my Gucci bag.

"Okay, stay safe and don't do nothing I wouldn't do because you know I'm a hoe," laughed Charlotte, pulling me into a hug, letting out a light laugh.

"I won't."

They followed me out of my room, and I went to KJ's room, pushing the door open lightly, looking inside. Ever since Cassie got back home, she slept in the same bed as KJ, just like they did when they were younger. Even before all this happened, they only slept together when they were scared. I smiled, seeing KJ and Cassie hugged up with one another. Leaving the door half open for my sisters to hear them, I grabbed my keys from the rack and went outside to my car. Getting inside, I took a deep breath and cranked my car up, pulling out of the driveway. "Thursday" by Leven Keli blasted through the speakers of my car as I made my way to the new restaurant on 9th Avenue. I pulled back the top on my Mustang, enjoying the fall breeze brushing against my skin.

This shit ain't for nobody
Do this shit in private, yeah
Gotta be invited, yeah
On a Thursday night
On a Thursday night, yeah

Pulling into the semi-full parking lot, I spotted a parking spot close by and killed my engine, getting out. Making my way inside, I approached the host with a bright smile.

"Reservations for James."

"Of course, right this way."

She grabbed a menu and escorted me upstairs to a private area. When I got there, I saw Devon sitting at the table, typing away at his phone. Grabbing my menu from the host, I sent her on her way and approached Devon. I guess the sound of my heels clicking against the tile floors alerted him, making him look up. I took in his amazing appearance, and it seemed as if neither of us could stop smiling. He sported a white turtleneck, beige blazer, matching pants, and a pair of Dolce and Gabbana loafers.

His beard was shaped up nicely, and he looked like he got a fresh fade. He stood up and approached me, bringing me into a hug. I inhaled the scent of his Creed Aventus cologne, and I immediately drenched my underwear. There was something about a man who smelled good that drew me in like a crackhead.

"You look gorgeous."

"You look handsome yourself." I smiled lightly.

I stood back as he pulled my chair out for me. Once I was seated, he sat in front of me, still smiling like a little kid at a candy factory.

"How you been?" he asked, tracing his tongue across his plump, even-toned lips.

"I've been good, just trying to get myself back together."

"Nothing wrong with that; how're your kids?"

"They're doing good. It's been a minute."

"It has. I'm glad you took me up on my offer."

"Of course, we haven't talked in a minute."

"So, how's work? I recently saw that you were at the VMAs this year."

"It's going good, but it could be better."

"What? Dude, you literally work around celebrities," I laughed.

"Sometimes when you get into the limelight, sweetheart, everything starts to look the same. The same celebrities we see on TV and social media aren't as exciting to be around as you'd think."

"Hmm, you make a point."

"How're the books going? I know you said you were taking a break from writing last time we talked."

"I'm still taking a break."

"Damn, I could really use some new content from you."

"What you mean?"

"Well, while I was busy after work, I stayed up late reading your book. You got yourself a new reader — shit, a fan at that."

The mention of having a new fan of my work sounded amazing in the beginning, but after everything that transpired with Tykell, having a fan of my work sounded like some stalker shit now. I calmed my nerves, hoping he didn't catch the sudden change in my demeanor. The last thing I wanted to do was ruin my date based on my past experiences.

"So, what did you read first?"

"Your series *Chocolate Kisses & Dark Surprises.*"

"Oh, that's a throwback," I smiled.

"Thought I would start with your old stuff before moving on up to your new stuff."

"So, what do you think?"

"I think you sex scenes could use a bit of work," he smiled, messaging the hair on his chin.

"What? Oh no, see, you must not be reading the right work because my scenes are bomb."

"Ehh, it could use a lil' more work. I mean, yeah, what you wrote was aight if you into that amateur Dreampen smut they used to write back in the day."

"Wow, you really offended me. Just when I thought you were cute," I laughed.

"Take it as constructive criticism. You did your thing. I'm not even gonna lie, your book is dope. You dangerous with that pen, Queen, I do give you that."

"So, what do you suggest I do to improve my sex scenes?" I asked, tilting my head to the side, staring into his perfect hazel eyes.

"I don't wanna run you away," he laughed, shaking it off.

"You won't."

"Trust me, I will."

We talked and laughed for what seemed like hours while enjoying fine cuisine. We started getting closer, and I felt like I was on cloud nine by the time it was time for us to go. We stayed in the restaurant conversing as if it didn't have to close soon. After deciding that it was time to leave the restaurant, we walked around the park, still not running out of shit to talk about. We talked about our dreams, aspirations, goals, and our future. I felt like it'd been a while since I had an intellectual conversation with someone and connected with them on a deeper level. Even with my heels doing a number on my feet, I still didn't want the night to end. We were currently at Bryant Park, eating ice cream, talking about 90s shows. I knew my sisters were gonna get the wrong idea since I told them I would be home at one and it was going on three in the morning.

"This is the first time I've ever heard a man tell me that they like *The Parkers*," I laughed.

"You must not be around the right men. *The Parkers* was my show growing up. I have a few sisters, so you know I had to let them watch what they wanted to. We grew up in the hood, so we had to share the living room TV. We didn't have money like that for a TV to go in everybody room. Shit, if my sisters wanted to watch *The Powerpuff Girls*, my big ass had to sit there and watch it with them."

"I can't relate," I laughed.

"Of course, you can't."

"What's that supposed to mean?"

"You look like that type to be privileged."

"I won't take offense; I was kinda privileged."

"I knew you were," he laughed lightly, twirling his tongue around his ice cream. I almost nutted up watching his tongue do things I'd never seen anyone do. Clearing my throat and quickly looking away, I finished my ice cream sandwich.

"Well, this was fun while it lasted, but I gotta go."

"That's fine. Me too; I have to work tomorrow."

He grabbed my hand and escorted me to my car. Once we reached my car safely, I looked up at him, gazing into his eyes again.

"I really had fun tonight. Like, I haven't been out on a date in God knows how long."

"Same here, I'm really happy I got to get some of your time."

"Maybe we can do this again sometime."

"Most definitely. I'll call you. And don't be a stranger," he replied, pulling me into a hug. I was praying he didn't feel my nipples that were hard as pebbles poking up against his chest. We slowly let go of one another before staring into one another's eyes for what seemed like the thousandth time tonight. He grabbed my chin and lifted it up as I stood on my toes. Even with heels on, I puckered my lips up. As soon as his lips were about to touch mine, my phone started ringing. We both let out a nervous sigh before laughing.

"That's probably my sisters."

"It's fine, call me."

"I will," I laughed lightly.

He opened my car door for me and helped me inside before closing it. I could do nothing but smile the entire drive home. The way I was smiling, you would have thought I just had the best dick of my life.

Chapter 12: Made 4 You

The entire drive to my house, all I had in my head was Celeste's infectious laugh, the way her beauty lightened the entire room, and the way that dress hugged all her curves in the right places. When I pulled into my yard, I sighed seeing Serenity's baby blue 2020 Jeep Wrangler sitting nice and pretty on the side. She was leaned up against her car, wearing nothing but a pair of silk, pastel pink shorts, a Gucci sweatshirt, a pair of black Uggs, and her hair was tucked into her custom-made bonnet that had pictures of her on it. I could tell by the unpleased look on her face that she was here for one reason. I decided to ignore all incoming calls tonight so that I could give Celeste my undivided attention. Getting out of my car, I sighed approaching her.

"What you doin' here, Serenity?" I asked.

"Thought somebody done killed your ass because it's not like you to ignore my calls. So, what's going on, Devon?"

"Ain't nothing going on. I was busy."

"At three in the morning?" she replied, sucking her teeth and looking at her Apple watch.

"I know what time it is, Ren."

"Where were you?"

"Why you quizzin' me like I'm a criminal?"

"Because you come back looking like a hoe, ignoring my calls, and you acting like this shit is normal with us when you know we don't do that."

"I'm not in the mood to do this with you right now. Look, I had a good ass day, and I'm tired," I replied, letting out a yawn. She raised one eyebrow at me before approaching and sniffing me.

"Why you smell like a bitch?" she quizzed.

"Do I ask you why you smell like a nigga when we get together? No, I don't, so don't do that. Are you my best friend right now? Or are we fuck buddies? Because I do wanna tell you how my day went."

She looked hesitant and rolled her eyes. Then, she let out a sigh.

"I'm your best friend," she replied, shaking her head.

"Good, now come on, it's cold out here. Dressed like you about to beat somebody ass."

"I thought I had to beat your ass," she laughed lightly.

She followed me to my front door and watched me unlock it. Opening it and letting her inside first, I followed her, and we went to my kitchen. Heading to my fridge, I grabbed a bottle of Fiji water and passed it to Serenity before leaning on the counter, facing her to see she had a skeptical look on her face.

"I went on a date." I said plainly.

"Oh really?" she replied, tilting her head to the side, trying to be funny.

"Yes really. Be nice."

"I am being nice."

"Right."

"Did you have fun?"

"I did." I smiled just thinking about tonight.

"Smiling pretty hard. Who was your lil' date? Must not have been a quick fling because I didn't see anyone with you when you pulled up."

"Don't worry about who she is."

"Why not? I might like her. We might can do a lil' threesome," she laughed.

"You got jokes."

"I always do. Now the real question is, what made you start dating again?"

"It wasn't something that I thought about. I just haven't talked to her in a minute and decided that I wanted to take her out."

"Hmm, is she cute? You gotta show me a picture of her."

"I'm not telling you who she is, at least not yet. You don't like being on your best behavior."

"I'll be nice, I told you that."

"I'll tell you when I'm ready."

"Okay, I respect that. Date must have been good if you skinning and grinning in here."

"It was great. I don't think I've connected with someone on that type of level in a long time."

"Oh, is that so?" she asked, getting sensitive.

"I didn't mean it like that."

"How did you mean it?"

"You know we connect on a different level. You been my dawg since day one, Ren. It's just, I'm getting older and you know Moms and the fam be getting on my ass about finding somebody and starting a family. You know I don't feed into that shit regardless, but after my date tonight, I realized how fun it is to be out there again. And just from the conversations me and her had, I never knew it felt so good to connect verbally instead of sexually. I mean, she fine as hell, body banging, pretty face, she the whole package, but it's like something different about her. She's not like those other females I come across onset or at those parties. She's something else."

"Wow. One date with her and you ready to start a family."

"It's not like that."

"I kinda think it's a waste of time."

"Why is that?"

"Look, you have a lot going on right now. You even said it yourself, you don't have time for a family or a relationship. You wanna further your career, right? Come on. And dating takes a long time, especially when you wanna find the right person."

"You're right about furthering my career. I'm just at the point to where whatever happens, happens."

"Just look at me and what we got going. I'm rich, I have men kissing my feet, and I have you. You're my best friend and you're my fucking lover. Devon, you can improve your career and keep doing what we're doing."

"We can't do this forever, Ren."

"How about we make it official then?"

"You know we can't do that."

"Why not?"

"You know why."

"Well, for now, let's just make the best of it. I've been so busy with work and other shit, and I'm exhausted. You wanna rub me down?"

"You can rub me down."

"How about we take turns," she replied, hopping down from her stool and walking over to me, throwing her arms around my shoulder. I gripped a handful of her ass, looking down at the huge smile she had on her face.

"You know I love you, no matter who comes in the picture, right?" she said.

"And I love you through any disagreement we have," I replied, picking her up and carrying her to my bedroom. Even though I knew I had to go to sleep soon, I thought that I might as well tire the both of us out in the bedroom instead of just waiting to fall asleep. Serenity was something else, and even after our conversation, I didn't take anything she said to heart. I knew she was speaking to me as a fuck buddy because she was still pissed off that I was ignoring her calls. Serenity and I had that type of relationship where we could talk to one another about any and everything.

We could talk to one another about the relationships we got into and give honest feedback without being biased. I knew better than to have this conversation with her tonight knowing she would say any and everything to keep another woman out of my head — even if that meant drowning me in her pussy until I couldn't get out. I knew she would want to have this conversation with me again in the morning when it was a new day and our judgement wasn't clouded.

Even after fucking each other's brains loose, I still couldn't get Celeste out of my mind. And it wasn't even in a sexual way. How many niggas you know could say that they couldn't get a woman out of their head in a non-sexual way? It was six in the morning, and I had Serenity knocked out on my chest. I looked up at the mirror above my head and sighed. I was confused and that was a first when it came to Serenity. She may have joked around about wanting to get in a relationship, but I couldn't do that. Shit was already off with us fucking now; I couldn't get with her. I knew that God made certain people for one another, but I didn't know if He made Serenity to be my woman, or if He made Celeste for me. I had to be patient I had to see what this woman was really about to know for sure what God had in store for me.

Chapter 13: Picking Up the Pieces

Celeste

As much as I would have wanted her to, Cassie still wouldn't come out of this bubble she was in. It had gotten to the point where she wouldn't talk to me or her father. She either had KJ ask us what she wanted or she would text me. When I tried to talk to her, she gave me one-word answers until I backed off and left her alone.

I asked her therapist for suggestions on getting her to open up. She kept telling me that she would talk when she was ready. I understood that I had to be patient with her, but I desperately wanted my little girl back. I was beginning to wonder if I would ever get her back.

Other than my date with Devon a couple weeks ago, I'd been staying home. Cassie refused to leave the house, so I stayed in with her, hoping she would randomly decide to talk. I felt myself going crazy, so I asked Kadarius to come stay with the kids while I went out for a few hours. It was the least he could do. Lately, he hadn't been doing much with the kids. KJ wouldn't leave Cassie's side, and Kadarius used that as an excuse to not do anything. It was a bunch of bullshit if you'd ask me. He could at least have a movie night with them. Though I hated the sight of him, I allowed him to stay at my house every now and then to make Cassie feel better.

When Kadarius got to the house, I grabbed my purse, keys, and laptop. Over the last few days, random storylines had been popping in my head. I decided to start a new book. When I got to the coffee shop, I was surprised to see that they weren't busy despite it being lunch time. After arriving and ordering my favorite coffee, I found a table, sat down, and cracked open my laptop. Immediately, my fingers took over the keyboard, and I zoned out.

Two thousand words later, I got knocked out of my trance by the sound of my phone ringing. It was Devon.

"Hey, Beautiful! How are you today?"

"I'm good. At the coffee shop, getting some writing done. How about you?"

"Doing good now that I hear you are back writing. What brought this on?"

I explained to him how storylines had been popping up in my head. He told me he was happy for me and asked if he could swing by to see me since he was in the area. I agreed and hung up. Ten minutes later, he was coming through the door. I stood up and hugged him. He kissed me softly on my cheek. It was just a peck, but it was enough to make my hormones rage. I can't remember the last time I had sex. I'm sure my pussy had cobwebs by now.

"What have you been up to?" I asked after we sat down.

"I had some meetings this morning. Just got done and decided to come out for lunch. You came across my mind, so I decided to call and check on you. Haven't seen you since our date."

"I've been thinking about you too. Been wanting to see you, but my daughter seems to be falling into a depression, so I've been home."

"I'm sorry to hear that. What is the therapist saying?"

I explained to him that the therapist told me that Cassie would open up when she's ready, and how I thought that was a bunch of bullshit. He slightly agreed.

"I do think she will come to you when she's ready, however, I think I know something that might help. Have you ever heard of a smash room?"

"I haven't. What is it?"

He told me a smash room was a place people go to let out their anger. They put on protective gear and smash things, such as furniture. It sounded like a great idea to me. The hard part would be getting Cassie to leave the house.

"Didn't you say she listens to her brother?" Devon asked me.

"She does," I replied.

"Get him to convince her."

I looked up the information for the smash house and sent it to KJ, asking if it was something he would want to do. A few minutes later, he replied that he would. I told him to ask Cassie if she would come. This time, he took longer to text back. My guess was that he was trying to talk Cassie into it. I made conversation with Devon while I waited for him to reply. After what seemed like forever, he texted back and told me that Cassie had agreed to go.

"She's going!" I told Devon excitedly.

"Great, I hope it works out."

We talked for a little while longer before he left so that I could get back to writing. I wrote another three thousand words before going home. On the way there, I prayed that the smash room would give Cassie the breakthrough she needed.

The next day

"Are you guys ready to have some fun?" I asked KJ and Cassie while we were on the way to the smash room.

"I am, mom," KJ told me.

Cassie didn't say anything. I was beginning to question if asking her to come out the house was a good idea. I quickly dismissed the thought because I knew something had to be done. Once we got there, we went inside, and I signed all of the necessary paperwork. After we put on our safety gear, we listened to instructions from the clerk before entering our room.

"So, we're just supposed to hit stuff?" KJ asked me.

"Yep, we just hit stuff."

He was about to say something but was cut off by the sound of Cassie smashing an old TV that was in the room.

"Ahhh!" she screamed as she hit the TV over and over again.

"That's right, baby. Let it out. Come on, KJ, let's get to it."

KJ and I started smashing random things in the room. It felt good as hell too. At some point, I imagined Kadarius's head on one of the TVs I hit. I also imagined myself hitting Tykell a few times.

"Why didn't you come for me?" Cassie yelled.

"What was that sweetheart?" I asked her.

"Why didn't you or Daddy come for me? You do all that talk about how your job is to protect us, but you didn't come for me!"

I immediately broke down in tears at her revelation.

"Sweetie, we looked everywhere for you! There wasn't a day that went by where I wasn't out searching."

"Well, you didn't look hard enough. I had to deal with that man touching me every night and that woman trying to make me call her Mommy. I prayed to God that you and Dad would find me. There were even times I prayed that I wouldn't wake up the next day."

She continued to smash as she talked. I looked over at KJ, and he was just standing there looking just as shocked as I was.

"Cassie, sweetheart..."

"No! You've been wanting me to talk; now I'm talking. I went through hell. The only reason I'm home is because that woman decided to bring me back. You and Daddy had nothing to do with it. I keep hearing you say that you got me back. Well, you didn't get me back. I was dropped off on the porch. Why didn't you come for me? Why? Why? Why?"

All this time, I had been wanting my daughter to tell me how she felt and now that she was, I wished I hadn't pushed her. Knowing that she felt the way she did about me and her father hurt my soul. What made matters worse, was that there was nothing I could do to fix it. As much as I wanted to turn back time and change what happened, the reality was that I couldn't. The only thing I could do was try to assure my child that nothing like this would happen to her again.

I put down the sledgehammer I had in my hand, walked over to Cassie, and took her in my arms. We both cried for the next five minutes before I spoke.

"Listen to me. Both of you, listen and you listen good. As

long as I have breath in me, nothing will ever happen to you again. If I have to stay at home with you for the rest of my life, then so be it."

"I don't want you to stop your life, Mommy. I'm just having a hard time getting over this. In a way, I feel betrayed by you and Daddy. I'm sure it will go away. I just don't know when."

"Take all the time you need, sweetheart. I'm not going anywhere. Do you want to stay awhile longer, or are you ready to go?"

"I want to stay. Thanks for bringing me here."

She started smashing things again, and for a moment, I just watched her. I made a mental note to thank Devon for suggesting this. I prayed to God that He would remove all of the anger from my child.

Chapter 14: She's Not Mine

"Kadarius, I'm not about to sit here and argue with you," Celeste stressed.

"All I asked was where you were going," I sighed.

"That's none of your business. Do I ask you where you be going when I have the kids? No I don't, so don't do that."

"We have kids together; I need to know your whereabouts in case of an emergency."

"No, you want to know my whereabouts so you can be nosey. I have a phone and so do the kids in case there is an emergency. Look, I gotta go," she replied, trying to walk off, but I pulled her back in by her arm, raising one of my brows at her. She was dressed in a red sundress with a pair of black heels, and her hair was flowing freely down her back like a river. I couldn't remember the last time I'd seen her dress this way. Part of me felt as if she was seeing someone else, and I didn't like that shit one bit.

"You seeing someone?" I asked, deciding to get the question out of the way before it wrecked my brain like a wrecking ball.

"And if I was?" she shrugged, pulling her arm from my grasp.

"I need to know."

"No, you don't need to know."

"Yes, I do. I need to know who's around my kids."

"He's not around our kids," she sighed.

"So, you are seeing someone." I laughed cold heartedly.

"Bye, Kadarius."

When she tried to walk off again, I grabbed her once more. She let out a loud sigh before yanking her arm away again.

"What do you want?" she asked with annoyance laced all throughout her voice.

"I want you. I want us to stop this cat and mouse game, Celeste. We've been together for way too long to throw what we have away. We've been through way too much to let what we have together go. I love you," I replied, feeling that hurt I felt every night knowing that she was no longer mine.

"If you loved me, you would have never played me the way you did. If you cared about me, you would have never been so selfish to think about only yourself."

"Celeste, I —."

"Fuck you. We're through. You cheated on me. You didn't care about my feelings or your family. Kadarius, we had everything going right for us, everything. But you fucked it up over some dick. I thought we were going to be forever when I met you, but I guess you fooled me then too. I'm never going to be anyone's fool again, and I'll make sure of that. I will no longer be your fool, Tykell's fool, or anyone."

"You weren't a fool. You're telling me you don't feel anything for me anymore? You don't feel that spark we had? You don't feel anything? We have a family together. I'm not justifying my actions, but people cheat, people have issues in their relationship, and they work together to fix them. We can fix us."

"There's nothing to fix. I don't feel anything. And it wasn't just you cheating on me. You cheated on me with a fucking man! A man, KD! A fucking man! You talked down on me and pushed your family to the side for some dick. I want you to feel exactly how I felt, but too bad, you're heartless. And like I said, I don't feel anything, unlike you. I don't like dick in my ass. The old Celeste, who you thought would push shit to the, side is gone. Go play with your kids; don't fucking play with me. Goodnight, Kadarius." she said, turning on her heels to walk over to her car. I watched as her car sped down the road, and I didn't even notice that I was crying until my tears rolled down my cheek and hit my lip.

I wasn't crying because she dogged me out. I was crying

because what she spoke was facts. I was crying because my family was no longer together anymore.

"Daddy, you wanna watch a movie with us?" asked KJ. I quickly wiped my tears and turned to him with a huge smile on his face.

"Yeah son, what we watching?" I asked, coming in and closing the door.

"The Mask."

"The Mask? I thought you didn't like that movie."

"Cassie wanna watch it, so I'll watch it."

"That's nice of you. How's she holding up?"

"She's good. We went to this place to hit stuff. She and Mommy started crying. I don't know what was going on, but I know after that, she was back to herself."

"I'm happy she's back to herself. I'll be in the living room in a few. Go and keep your sister company, okay?"

"Okay," he smiled, running off.

I headed to my bedroom, making sure to lock the door. Reaching in my pocket, I pulled out my phone to make a call. I sighed in relief, hearing that I got a response.

"Hey, how you doin'?" asked Lemarcus.

"Not good."

"Wassup?"

"Celeste is seeing someone else."

"What?"

"I lost her, man," I sniffled.

"You didn't lose her. The both of you still have kids together. Come on, man. You act like she hates you."

"She does. I thought I could talk her into getting back to where we used to be, but she's not budging. I love her, man. I really do, but she doesn't love me anymore."

"Then it's time to leave her alone. She's been through a lot, Kadarius. You did cheat on her, and Lord knows what that psycho did to her when he kidnapped her. Celeste is just trying to get back into the groove of things. She's trying to live her life after what she went through. I think you need to do the same. I know you don't like talking about this, but go out there and find a new man or woman. Find whatever the hell you're into. I know you told me it was out of curiosity, but —."

"I didn't call you to judge me; I called you for advice."

"And I'm giving you advice. She's not yours anymore, man. Drop it. Aren't you with your kids right now? Try to improve your relationship with them. I know your daughter is back with you. Try to bond with her. Stop worrying about Celeste when she's not worrying about you. You got bigger issues to handle; stop stressing."

"She's mine," I replied, hanging up.

Dialing my sister's number, I called her over to babysit the kids. I needed time alone to think and process what the hell I needed to do before I lost Celeste forever. Walking over to my dresser, I pulled out a small box that once held my Rolex and pulled out a small bag. Opening it, I placed a little bit of the white substance on my finger before snorting it, feeling that rush kick in. I fell back on my bed and looked up at the ceiling fan, watching it spin, feeling the world spin around me.

"She's not yours." Lemarcus's voice echoed through my head.

She is mine, I said to myself.

Once my sister was over, I rushed out of the door, not even bothering to say anything to her or my kids. I found myself at a male strip club, spending two thousand, maybe even more. I needed something to get Celeste off of my mind, even if it meant this.

Chapter 15: Sativa

I watched as Celeste swayed to the beat of the music blasting softly through my apartment with a cup of lemonade in her hand. I was laid back in my chair as she danced to almost every song that played off of my playlist. I couldn't do anything but laugh at how excited she got after every song changed to another. Apparently, my playlist was right up her alley because every song that played was "her song".

"You always this free?" I asked, licking my lips.

"You got a banging ass playlist. I'm always free when I'm listening to music."

"Has anyone ever told you that your presence is enough to make a man lose his mind?"

"I'm flattered," she smiled, coming over and placing her half empty cup on the coaster.

"I'm serious. I mean, we've been seeing each other long enough for me to get this comfortable with you."

"You're right. I don't know how many times I can tell you how attracted I am to you."

"Well, I'm glad we're attracted to each other," I laughed lightly with hooded eyes.

"Don't think I'm judging you before I ask you this."

"What's good?"

"You seem high," she laughed lightly, nudging my shoulder.

"I'm not even gonna lie to you. I am. I smoked some sativa before you came over. I know it's a little disrespectful to invite you over while I'm like this, but I've been stressed out and tired from work."

"You're totally fine. Sativa, huh?"

"Yeah," I replied, with my eyes still half shut, staying in my zone but still clinging to reality enough to pay attention to Celeste.

"Got any left?"

"Yeah, why?"

"I wanna hit," she replied, placing her hand on top of mine. I quickly removed her hand and cleared my throat while getting up. It was no lie that Celeste's sex appeal had a nigga with blue balls every time she was over, but I didn't want her to think I wanted her just for sex. I wanted her for her mind and soul. Her body was just a plus. Shit, just hearing her say she wanted a hit, had my mind in the gutter.

"Why do you always do that?" she scoffed with her arms crossed.

"Do what?"

"Move away from me whenever we touch."

"You said you wanna hit the blunt, right?" I asked, disregarding her question.

"Really?"

"Yeah, I got some rolled up already."

"Not that, answer me."

"I'll answer you later."

She followed me into my bedroom, and I could tell by the look on her face she was taking in my decor. From the smile on her face, I could tell she was impressed by how well everything was decorated. I walked into my walk-in closet and pulled out my box of weed, grabbing two pre-rolled blunts and my custom-made torch lighter. Taking a seat on my bed, I waved for her to take a seat next to me. Since the rain messed up the date I originally had planned for us, we were stuck in my house, watching movies, listening to music, and taking in one another's presence. I had on a pair of grey sweats and a Nike graphic tee with a pair of Nike slides. I knew Celeste felt a little overdressed since she wore a sundress and heels. I handed her the blunt and watched as she placed it in between her plump lips that were covered in glittery lip gloss. She inched close to my face, waiting for me to light the tip. Doing just that, I watched as she took a long pull from the blunt. Never had I seen a woman smoke a blunt as sexily as Celeste. We both laid back on the bed, staring up at the mirror on my ceiling.

"So, answer the question," she said, passing me the blunt.

"What question?"

"Damn, you that buzzed?" she laughed, rolling her eyes.

"Trust me, after you finish you're gonna be just as buzzed as me, baby girl."

"Why every time we touch, you run away from me?"

"You want the truth?"

"Yes," she replied, looking over at me.

"Because I want you."

"You want me?"

"Look, I'm high as hell and I get real blunt when I'm high. So, whatever I say, just remember. I'm under the influence."

"We're both grown; speak your mind."

"I wanna do things to you that I know you won't let me do. But I don't want you to think I just want you around for sex. I love your personality and the type of person you are. It's just, the more I see you, the more my urges grow."

"Wow."

"Wow what?" I asked, taking a pull from the blunt and passing it back to her.

"There's nothing wrong with expressing that. Trust me, there have been plenty of times that I've imagined doing things to you too," she replied, trying to hide the embarrassment on her face.

"You do?"

"I do."

"Damn, I don't know what to say."

"You expected that reaction out of me?" she laughed. I knew the weed was getting to her due to the change in her demeanor and the way her body quickly relaxed.

"No, I didn't to be honest."

"So how about we play twenty-one questions? We're both

fucked up, so I doubt we'll remember what either of us said."

"You got that right."

"You go first."

"Okay. What's your dream job, if you're not already living it?"

"I wanna be a pornstar."

"What?" she laughed, shaking her head and looking over at me.

"Nah, for real. I mean, I'm already a director. I know this is your first time hearing me speak about my other job. This is something most people don't know about me. I film a lot of videos; I just wanna be in front of the camera one day."

"What's stopping you?"

"Judgement."

"So what? I think you should do it. If it's something you really wanna do, you go for it no matter what."

"I wish it was that easy."

"Do you know how many people bashed me and told me that "writing isn't a career; it's a hobby"? How many people shitted on my dream? Half of them motherfuckers out there reading my work while masturbating to it. I'm one hell of an author; I give myself that. Follow your dreams."

"I appreciate that."

"It's nothing. I wish people would have told me to follow my dreams growing up. I would have probably gone further."

"I think you're a great author too."

"Thank you. Your turn."

"Don't judge me."

"I'd never."

"In almost every novel of yours that I've come across, I see that you've mentioned a threesome."

"Oh, God," she laughed.

"What?"

"Nothing. I always write about it but never go into full detail because I've never had one before."

"Do you wanna have one?"

"With who?"

"Who do you think?"

Her response got interrupted by my ringing phone. Digging into my pocket, I pulled out my phone and saw that Ren was calling me. Hitting decline and turning my phone off, I cleared my throat, deciding to change the subject, not wanting to scare her away.

"What makes you so attracted to me?" I asked.

"That's a dumb question."

"How?"

"Have you not seen yourself? Devon, you fine as hell. Why wouldn't I be attracted to you?"

"Give me details."

"Okay. Your body is beyond any woman's dreams and your skin is damn near perfect. How the hell you got clear skin and I break out almost every day? Your smile is amazing
and —"

She stopped mid- sentence, looking over at me, licking her lips. Catching me by surprise, she climbed on top of me and pressed her lips on mine. My hands roamed her plump, round ass as she ran her hands up my shirt, messaging my six pack. Pulling her dress up, I pulled away from the kiss, trying to catch my breath. I knew she felt the bulge in my pants poking at her inner thigh. She was over here trying to dry hump a nigga when I just wanted to pin her up against a wall and fuck all the common sense out of her brain. I wanted to fuck the religion and beliefs that she held out of her. Slipping my finger in her thong, I licked my lips and smiled with anticipation feeling how soaked she was. She leaned down to my ear and sucked on my earlobe before stopping to speak.

"I want you inside me," she whispered.

Is it hot in here or is it just me?

I'm so high in here, been smokin' on this weed

Told 'em, Go on, take a shot on three

Told 'em, Drinks is on me

Yeah, the drinks are on me

"Sativa" by Jhene Aiko and Swae Lee played softly throughout my room. I fingered her as her moans were like music to my ears. It was rare for me to come across woman with beautiful sex faces, especially in the line of work I was in. But this girl right here was a different breed. The faces she made, made a nigga wanna bust a nut even though I wasn't even inside of her yet.

"I see you started the party without me," said Ren, making Celeste jump off of me and shriek in shock. She quickly stood up and fixed herself, trying to figure out how the hell Serenity got in here. I watched as Ren circled Celeste like a shark circling its prey.

"Hi, I'm Serenity, Devon's best friend. But they call me Ren. I've heard so much about you," she smiled, touching Celeste's hair.

"It's nice meeting you. I was just leaving."

"Oh, you don't have to leave. Don't let me interrupt. My best friend was sure right about one thing. You are beautiful. It's the body for me," she smiled, eyeing Celeste down like a nigga would.

"I have to get going; it was nice meeting you, Ren." Celeste replied, trying to walk off but Serenity grabbed her, making me get up.

"Let her go, Serenity."

"I just wanted to ask her something."

Serenity brought her lips to Celeste's ear, whispering to her before Celeste ran out the door like she was being chased by the feds. I sighed in annoyance at Serenity's behavior. She approached me and looked up with a satisfied look on her face. She grabbed my hand before sticking the same fingers I had inside of Celeste in her mouth. I watched as she moaned, licking her juices off of my fingers. If my hard dick didn't go limp from her busting in here, it was sure as hell back standing at attention now.

"No wonder you like her. She's a *sweet* girl. She should be coming back soon, real soon."

"And how do you know that? I wasn't ready for you to

meet her yet, and this is exactly why. What the hell did you say to her?"

"You know I'm full of surprises. Just know, she'll be back I gave her an offer that no woman would decline."

Chapter 16: A Muse in Her Feelings

"She asked you to do what now?!" exclaimed Charlotte.

"I don't even wanna repeat it; I'm embarrassed," I replied, pulling my covers over my head.

"Girl, please. With all the filthy shit you write in those books, you over here squirming like a lovesick schoolgirl over getting fingered," said Laurel, pulling the covers off of my head.

"Yeah, I know, but still. Shit, I thought I was a freak. I ain't got shit on these motherfuckers."

"So, stop acting like a little ass baby and tell us what was said," groaned Angela.

"I was high, okay? We almost had sex, then his best friend walked in on us. I don't know if this heffa was gay or what, but she was all up on me."

"Did you rock her shit?" asked Charlotte."

"No."

"Why not? Did you like it?"

"No."

"Then why?"

"I don't know, Charlotte, damn!"

"You must have liked it."

"I'm not gay, though."

"Don't call it gay, call it experimenting. I thought you always wanted to try those freaky acrobatic threesome shits you be writing about."

"Yeah, with my husband, but we know how that's going."

"So, what did she say?"

"*I see the way he looks at you. I know you want him and we both know he wants you. I thought it was too good to be true when he told me about you. You're beautiful, and I want him to experi-*

ence how good it would be to have the woman he's falling for and the woman he loves wrapped in one another. Come to 346 Ackerman Street if you wanna talk more. I know you want him inside you, and I wanna see how you taste personally she said it in a sweet, dangerous tone — like velvet.

"She wants to have a threesome with me and him," I replied, keeping the details at bay.

"I think you should do it," said Charlotte, causing all eyes to turn to her.

"What? No. I'm not having a threesome with a girl I don't know."

"It's not with just her, it's with Devon. We all know you got the feels for that nigga."

"I'm with CeCe I don't think she should do this," said Angela, with an uneasy face.

"Look, I've had a threesome before," Charlotte replied, catching everyone off guard.

"Spill it. How was it?"

"Girl, I couldn't walk right for a month, and I'm not even gay, but I wanted that bitch to eat me out like it was her last supper again. They did this lil' weird thing to my booty hole that —."

"Aye! Uh uh! That's enough!" I yelled covering my ears.

"I want somebody to do something to my booty hole," mumbled Laurel.

"Ain't nobody coming near my ass."

"Look, I think you'd enjoy it, really. If it's something you really wanna do, then do it. We all try new and spontaneous things in life. It's just a threesome, try it."

"I'll think about it."

"So, other than the creepy freak bitch who claims to be his best friend, what else happened on this little date? Learn anything new?"

I tucked my lips in, deciding to keep them out of my business. I knew I was high, but I wasn't high enough to forget that Devon told me that he filmed porn I didn't want them to think any less of his character because of his occupation because I wouldn't want anyone doing that to me. But learning new things and finding out a side of him that I wasn't aware of made me want to distance myself from him. I hated when my mind and body were at odds with one another. My common sense was telling me to stray away for a while to try and figure him out from a distance, but my body was telling me to show up to the address Serenity gave me in nothing but my finest lingerie with whipped cream, condoms, handcuffs, and a plan B pill.

"Nothing much, just the same old stuff."

"So, what you gonna do?" asked Angela.

"I don't know what I'm gonna do. I really like Devon, but this is too much for me. I don't know if I'm moving too fast or what. You both know what happened with Tykell."

"But Devon isn't him," said Laurel.

"How do you know? It's just that I don't wanna let my guard down and get taken advantage of. I've been through so much, and I've fought so hard to get where I am after that experience."

"I know, and this is why I want you to go through with it —to get over what happened and try new things. From what you tell us, Devon seems like a great guy. You've been talking to him for a few months now."

"He's such an amazing man. He even helped me get Cassie to open up, and I've tried everything to make that happen. He makes me laugh, and he gives me advice when I'm down. Guys, he's amazing. It's just, I don't wanna be fooled again. Devon is everything I want in a man, and I don't want that to all be a lie. He accepts me for me, and he supports and does things for me that Kadarius barely did throughout our entire marriage."

"Aww, just ride his dick into the sunset already, get the ring, and give me another niece or nephew," said Charlotte, jokingly fanning her eyes as if she was about to cry.

"Aww, he got you in your feelings and everything. Somebody really like him," teased Angela, nudging my shoulder.

"Shut up."

I pulled the covers over my head again, ignoring the girls taunting and teasing at me. I couldn't do anything but sit there and sit deep in thought on what Serenity said. I was curious, and I hated being curious, because I knew that sooner or later, I was gonna go searching to kill my curiosity.

Chapter 17: She's Still Mine

Kadarius

"This is all your fault, you know. If you hadn't come into my life, I would still have my family, that jackass wouldn't have kidnapped my daughter, and my wife wouldn't be going on dates with another man. I could have fought my urges had you not come along," I said to the ground.

Seeing Celeste dressed up to go out with another man still had me on edge. So much so, that I was in the backyard of our old house talking to Reggie's grave. I put a few sticks on the spot where I buried him so I would always remember exactly where he was. Every now and then, I would ride by the house. I told myself when I buried him that I would come out here and visit him sometimes because he hated being alone. Due to everything that happened with Cassie, this was the first time I had gotten the chance to.

It's crazy how I went from loving this man to hating his guts. When I found out he had nothing to do with Cassie's kidnapping, I felt guilty for killing him. Well, somewhat guilty. He might not have kidnapped my daughter, but he did make threats to my family. He and I were going to come to blows behind that alone. That didn't mean I was going to kill him, though.

Going back and forth about whether or not I should have killed him was irrelevant at this point. He was dead, and there was nothing I could do about it. I sat at Reggie's "grave" thinking about my next move. Reggie and that fucker, Tykell, may have been dead, but with Celeste seeing somebody new, I had a new enemy lurking. I needed to find out who he was. Since Celeste wouldn't tell me, I had to go to the next best source.

The next day

"Excuse me, miss, I'm looking for Charlotte Braxton."

"I'm not sure where she is. Let me page her for you."

If anybody knew who Celeste was seeing, it would be Charlotte. Those two told each other everything. I could have easily waited to talk to her at her house, but I figured I'd get a better response by popping up at her job. In my mind, she would tell me what I wanted to know just to get me out of her face. My phone started vibrating while I was waiting. It was Lemarcus. Not wanting to talk to him, I silenced the phone and put it back in my pocket. It started vibrating again, and when I checked, I noticed he was calling back. Part of me wondered if that was a sign that I shouldn't be doing this.

"Kadarius? What are you doing here? Something wrong with Celeste or the kids?" Charlotte asked, letting me know it was too late to change my mind.

"Oh no, everybody's good. I needed to ask you something."

"Umm...sure. What is it?"

"Who is he?"

"Who is who?"

"Don't play dumb with me, Charlotte. You know what I'm talking about."

"KD, I don't have time to play twenty-one questions with you. I'm on the clock. Now again I ask you, who is who?"

"The man Celeste is seeing."

Her eyes got big as saucers. I couldn't tell if they were big because she was shocked that I knew or shocked that I had the balls to ask. Either way, I had a feeling I was about to find out.

"I know like hell you didn't bring your ass to my job to ask me no bullshit like this. You and CeCe are not married anymore. Therefore, who she is or isn't seeing is not your business."

"Man, Charlotte, kill that noise and tell me what I want to know before we have a problem in here."

"Before we have a problem? Nigga, you must have forgotten who the fuck I am. I don't take kindly to threats. You can come in here trying to play the big bad wolf if you want to. You might huff and puff, but we all know you ain't about to blow nobody's house down."

She got loud with her last remark, so now her coworkers were staring at us. I didn't care, though. I came for some information, and I wasn't leaving until I got it.

"I really don't give a damn who you are. I just want to know who the nigga is entertaining my woman."

"Your woman? That's real cute, KD. We both know my sister isn't your woman anymore. Shit, from what I heard, you don't even like women anymore."

She had me there. There was nothing I could say, and she knew it. Everybody was standing there waiting on my response. The fact that she put my sexuality on front street was not cool.

"Nothing to say now, huh? Get the fuck out my face and don't ever come back to my job again. Can't believe you had the nerve to come to my job with this bullshit."

"Look, Charlotte, I..."

"I thought I told you to walk away. Are you still talking? No? Oh, 'cause I thought a nigga who stopped eating pussy to suck dick said something."

"We will finish this conversation later," I yelled before walking away.

"I look forward to it."

I guess coming to her job wasn't a good idea after all.

Chapter 18: Missing you

I'm not in love
It's just some kind of thing I'm going through
Goin' through, goin' through
And it's not infatuation
Ain't nothing goin' on between me and you
Me and you, me and you
But I dream about it every night, baby
Wanting you here with me
Making love to me
And oh

The sounds of Mary J's hit "Missing You" blasted through the speakers of my house as I cleaned it. Normally, I didn't listen to what I considered to be chick music, however, today Mary was speaking to me. The words she sang in this song describes exactly how I felt at the moment. It's been a little over a week since I have heard from Celeste. After Serenity burst in on us, she wouldn't take my calls. I've sent her several text messages begging her to speak to me, but they have all gone ignored.

Even though we weren't serious, not talking to her was hell. In such a short period of time, Celeste had grown on me. She was smart, beautiful, and fun to be around. She was also a good listener. I could tell her anything without the fear of being judged. In the short time we've known each other, she'd become my support system.

My phone rang, cutting my music off. I knew from the ringtone, it was Serenity. I let it go to voicemail like I had been doing for the last couple of days. She was the reason Celeste wasn't talking to me, therefore I wasn't talking to her. To my surprise, she didn't call multiple times like she usually does.

Right as Mary continued singing, my doorbell rang.

"Open this damn door, Devon!" I heard Serenity yell.

"Go away, Ren!"

"I will camp outside your house if I have to. Now open this fucking door."

Knowing she was serious, I let her in.

"What Serenity?" I screamed when I opened the door.

"Don't what me, Devon. Why haven't you been answering my calls?"

"You know why I haven't been answering your calls. You chased my woman away."

"Your woman? I thought the two of you were just friends."

"Whatever we were, we aren't anymore, and it's your fault."

"So, you playing me to the left for some chick? I been by your side since we met, and you mad at me about some random? Wow, Devon. Just wow."

"She isn't some random! We were developing feelings for each other. Who knows what we could have had if you hadn't run her away."

"Fuck you, Devon. You act like your feelings are the only ones that matter. What about mine?"

"What about yours?"

I really didn't give a shit about her feelings, but I decided to entertain her anyway.

"It doesn't take a genius to see that I'm in love with you. Every time I think we're getting closer, you bring another bitch around. Why is that?"

Every time I met a female I was feeling, Serenity and I had this same conversation. Don't get me wrong, Serenity was loyal as hell. However, she was too wild for me. She would have sex with anybody. Male or female. That wasn't the type of woman I wanted. I need a calm woman. Somebody who looks at her body as a temple. As much as Serenity told me she would change, I couldn't take it there with her. Not to mention, we were best friends for so long, I couldn't afford to take things to that level with her knowing what we already had going on.

"Ren, you know we not like that. Why you tripping?"

"I'm good enough to have sex with, but not good enough to be in a relationship with? Wow, Devon! Just wow!" Serenity yelled as tears slid down her face.

"Look, Ren, if us smashing every now and then is going to keep causing these kinds of problems, then maybe we need to chill. I got love for you, and there is nothing nobody can do to change that. However, I'll never be in love with you, and I need you to be okay with that."

"Damn, tell me how you really feel."

"I'm sorry, Ren."

"Keep your sorry, nigga."

I didn't respond, so she rolled her eyes before leaving and slamming my door. I hated breaking her heart, but it had to be done. My sights were set on one woman and woman only. That was Celeste Braxton.

Chapter 19: Thirsty

"Tell me anything, everything, whatever, I wanna hear. It's the sweet little nothings that's all I need to keep me here," I sang the lyrics to Jhene Aiko's song, "When We Love" as I drove.

After a lot of thinking, I decided that going along with what Serenity had requested was dead. I couldn't do that, no matter how strong my urges were. Today, I decided to have a self-care day. After everything that I've gone through, I took one self-care day out of the week. I went and got waxed, got thirty inches of Brazilian deep wave sewed in, got my nails and toes done, went to the spa, and I sat at the cafe and caught up on some reading. I was grateful that Charlotte was off today and kept the kids entertained. Since I was in such a good mood, I decided to cook the kids' favorite tonight. I planned on cooking smothered pork chops, garlic mashed potatoes, cornbread, and grilled asparagus. Since Walmart was right down the road, I went there. Parking my car and killing the engine, I got out and grabbed a cart. Going inside, I had one of my airpods plugged in my ear, letting my music still play softly. After grabbing everything I needed to grab, I sat in the horrendous self-checkout line, hoping that it would move quickly.

"Celeste?" someone called, making me turn around. When I turned around, I was face to face with the exact person I was trying to avoid.

"Serenity, right?"

"Right," she smiled, flipping her blonde bundles over her shoulder.

"I haven't seen you. I wonder why," she stated.

"Uh, I've been busy," I replied, trying to keep the conversation short.

"That's a shame. I've been wanting to see you."

"You have?"

"I have. I've been wanting to come to you and apologize."

"Apologize?"

"Yes. I was way out of line, and I know how much Devon really likes you. I feel as if I kinda ruined something that you two had going. I've always been an upfront person and I always say things without thinking. I never meant to make you feel uncomfortable. Devon is in the dumps without talking to you, and I thought that I should repair what I broke."

"Well, I accept your apology. You did come on quite strong. I just needed some space; I didn't know how to face him after you walked in on us."

"Girl, Devon ain't nobody for you to feel embarrassed. But I wanna start off on a new foot. Is that okay with you?" she asked, extending her hand.

Hesitant at first, I sighed and shook her hand. I grew uneasy, seeing her caress the top of my hand, so I pulled it away.

"Look, I'm not gay, just so you know," I said, making it known.

"I know. I'm sorry, you're just really beautiful. I'm not fully gay. I'm bi, just so you know."

"Oh okay," I laughed, shaking my head.

"So, what are your plans for the rest of the day?"

"Uh, well, my kids are going to be with my sister for the rest of the day, so I'll probably relax and catch up on American Horror Story."

"You have kids?"

"Yeah, twins."

"Aw, is that them?" she asked, pointing to my phone screen.

"It is."

"They're so beautiful. Well, I don't know about you, but sitting at home alone sounds boring. You should come over to my place and keep me company."

"I don't know."

"Come on, please? I was gonna go and do the same thing you were going to do, so we might as well keep each other company. Hey, and we can get to know each other."

"I don't know you like that to come over to your place."

"That's why you're coming over — to get to know me."

"I'm sorry, I'm gonna have to decline."

"Okay. What about if me, you, and Devon spend some time together? Or, I can just bring you to him and you guys can make up. I don't like seeing him down. You don't even gotta hang out with me; I just want him to see you."

"He misses me?"

"Like crazy. He's being a dick to me and everybody else because he thinks he screwed things up with you. I just wanna make things better."

"I don't know, Serenity."

"Please," she begged, poking her lip out. I looked hesitant before deciding that seeing Devon wouldn't hurt. Ignoring him for the past couple of days had been driving me crazy. I was so used to those good morning texts, good advice, and the laughs. I knew I should have approached the situation differently, but I wasn't thinking straight, and it was finally coming back to bite me in the ass.

"Okay, I'll come. Just because I miss him too."

"Aww, that's cute," she laughed.

"Yeah," I blushed, just thinking about seeing Devon.

"But after we get out of here, just follow me to his place. I have an extra key."

Nodding in agreement, I paid for my things and went to my car with her talking my head off. You would have thought that she and Devon were together by the way she talked about him. When I packed everything into my car, I followed her to Devon's place. When we got there, his car wasn't even in the driveway. I watched her get out of her car and wave for me to come over. Sighing, I got out and approached her.

"Are you sure it's a good idea to pop up on him unannounced?" I asked.

"I pop up on him unannounced all the time; it's fine. He's probably still at work," she replied, pulling a key from her pocket and walking inside with me following.

"Are you hungry?" she asked, going to his fridge.

"No, I'm fine. I ate already."

"Oh okay, so how serious are you and Devon?" she asked, hopping on top of the island and unscrewing the cap on her BLK water.

"I mean, it wasn't serious yet, but we were getting somewhere."

"Hm, he acting like y'all together. He gets attached real quick, so look out for that," she laughed.

"Oh, he does?"

"Yeah. Oh, and I read your book for the first time."

"Which one?"

"Velvet Dreams."

"Oh, I just put that out. How did you like it?"

"I loved it; it was really good. Shit, I don't even read books and that made me wanna pick up another. *Fifty Shades of Grey* ain't got shit on you."

"Thanks."

"For somebody who writes freak shit like that, I'm shocked that what I said scared you away."

"It just caught me off guard."

"Okay. Real shit, woman to woman, have you ever thought about having a threesome?"

"I have, but —."

"But what? Come on, Celeste. Look at you, look at me, and look at Devon," she said, hopping off the counter and coming towards me, sitting next to me.

"I don't know."

"Come on. You're telling me that you wouldn't enjoy Devon eating you out and me sucking on your t —."

"Uh, are you always this sexual with strangers?"

"I am."

"Wow, that's not good."

"I'm a pornstar."

"You're a what?"

"A pornstar, sweetheart. I'm naturally sexual."

"Wow, that explains a lot. Well, still, I don't know."

"Why? Is it because it's your first time? You nervous? What is it?"

"I'm not gay. No homo, you pretty and all, but I'm not into that lesbian shit."

"It's only one time, and if it's something you don't like, I can stop. There's nothing wrong with experimenting."

"I've never experimented with a woman."

She rolled her eyes before pressing her lips to mine, catching me off guard. I would have thought my natural instinct would have been to push her back and rock her shit, but I sat there and kissed her back. The taste of her pineapple lip gloss mixed with my lipstick left a savoring flavor. Her hands caressed my leg before slowly creeping up my dress. Finally snapping back into reality, I pulled away and got up, trying to conceal the tsunami that was forming in my underwear.

"Somebody's hot and bothered," she smiled, looking satisfied.

"Why the hell did you do that?"

"You didn't stop me."

Before I could reply, the front door opened, revealing a tired Devon. When he saw me, his face lit up.

"Celeste, what you doin' here?" he asked, walking up to me.

"Serenity invited me."

"She did?"

"Surprise?" smiled Serenity.

"She beat you up and brought you here? Ren can be a big ass bully who can't take no for an answer."

"No, it's fine. I wanted to see you."

"You did? I thought you were avoiding me."

"I was, and I wanna say sorry. I should have handled that situation better."

"You're fine."

"She sure is," mumbled Serenity, tracing her tongue over her bottom lip.

"Ignore her."

"I tried," I laughed.

"So Celeste, yes or no? This would be the perfect time," asked Serenity.

"What is she talking about?" asked Devon.

I looked Serenity in her eyes, still hesitant. It was as if my body was for it, but I was nervous. Thinking back to my conversation with Laurel and my sisters, I decided to take a risk.

"Yeah," I sighed.

"Yes! Okay, Devon stay here, we got a surprise for you, bestie," she smiled, pulling me by my arm into his bedroom and closing the door.

"I can't believe I'm doing this," I sighed, running my hands through my hair.

"You'll enjoy it. Now take off your dress."

"What?"

"Take off your dress. Or you want me to do it for you?"

Rolling my eyes, I took my dress off, leaving me in nothing but my Savage X Fenty blue, floral, lace lingerie.

"Damn," mumbled Serenity, walking circles around me.

"I see why he crazy over you," she smiled. Instead of just stripping down to her undergarments, she stripped completely, only wearing her bare skin. I was straight, and I couldn't help but to look at her body. Her ass was as plump as a melon, her waist was snatched, and her titties sat up so right, it looked like she got them done. She had a body any woman would kill for. Shit, including me. I didn't even notice that she called Devon inside. When he came in, he looked completely shocked. Before he could say anything, she strutted over to him and whispered something in his ear, making him look at me.

"You don't have to this. I know she can pressure people into shit, but if —."

"I wanna do it."

"You do?

"Yeah," I smiled, walking over to him.

"You not joking with me? You dead ass serious right now?"

"Yes, Devon." I laughed at how nervous he was, eyeing me down. I watched him unbutton his red Ralph Lauren polo, revealing that body I loved to stare at. He walked up and pressed his lips to mine, picking me up and carrying me to the king-size bed, laying me down on the soft, white, silk sheets. When he dropped his pants, his soldier was standing at attention.

I wanna kiss you, girl, I wanna kiss you

Girl, I wanna love you

Oh, am I moving too fast?

Fuck that (Well, well, well)

Your momma must have taught you well

'Cause you taste so purified

PARTYNEXTDOOR's song, "Thirsty" played through the speakers as a naked Serenity walked seductively over to us.

Devon spread my legs and pulled my panties down with his teeth while Serenity unclipped my bra, freeing my breasts. Devon kissed my inner thigh, making my body shudder. I didn't know what felt better — Devon kissing and licking in between my thighs or Serenity kissing and sucking on my breasts while caressing my abdomen. Failing to conceal my moan, I let one out once Devon's warm mouth attached itself to my clit, making me jump. This man was something serious. I didn't know whether to feel intimidated or turned on even more by watching him feast on my treasure while staring me in my eyes. Serenity grabbed me by my face and pressed her lips to mine. While Devon's long, thick tongue plunged in and out of me, Serenity tongue kissed me while playing with my clit.

"Fuck!" I yelled, trying to run from Devon, who was now giving me finger and tongue action. He held my waist steady, making sure I couldn't get away from him.

"Mmm, you like that?" asked Serenity, sucking and kissing on my neck. She brought her lips to my ear, while messaging my fully erect nipples.

"You like that? You want more?" she asked, nibbling at my earlobe.

"Yes! Oh, fuck, I'm about to cum!" I screamed, arching my back and gripping the sheets.

"Do it; cum for me," she spoke seductively, making me release all of my juices on Devon's face. My legs were shaking just from the head. Only the Lord knew what my ass would feel after he put the dick in.

I watched him come up and lick my juices off of his plump lips, as it also covered his beard. Serenity pulled him up by his chin and kissed him passionately, moaning his name. I fingered myself as I watched him tongue her down, and she stroked his manhood over me.

"Shit," he hissed, as she jacked him to perfection.

He moved her hand before getting in between my legs and placing the tip at my entrance. I was so caught off guard when he placed both of my legs on his shoulders and eased himself in. I winced in pain, trying to get accustomed to his size. Not only was he blessed with ten inches, but he was thicker than a bowl of cold grits. Once I was fully adjusted to his size, he delivered slow, deep strokes, making me grip the sheets once more. Serenity held my arms down to keep me from gripping them.

"You so tight," he groaned, picking up his pace.

"Mm, fuck harder," I moaned.

"You want it harder?" he asked, pounding my shit. He was fucking me so hard, I almost lost all my common sense.

"Fuck, I'm finna cum!" I screamed, feeling my orgasmic high rush in.

"Cum on this dick, baby. Cum for me," he said, going deeper.

I came so hard, I almost fucked around and passed out. My legs shook violently as he still punished my shit.

"I'm about to cum too," he hissed, pulling out. I was still in the midst of catching my breath when I saw Serenity catch his load in her mouth, deep throating him.

We were at this for three hours straight, and even with me

on the brink of death from pleasure they still continued like the Energizer Bunny. I knew for a fact that when I woke up from this, I wouldn't be able to walk straight for months.

Chapter 20: No More Mr. Nice Guy

It'd been a couple weeks since I popped up on Charlotte at her job and I still had no clue who Celeste was seeing. After failing with her, I asked the kids some general questions to see if they knew anything, but that was a bust. Using my kids to get information on their mother was wrong, and I felt bad about it afterwards. I had to try, though. I needed to know who my competition was.

Celeste asked me to drop the twins off at a birthday party for her so she could meet Charlotte and Laurel for dinner. When I picked them up, I overheard Celeste tell Cassie that they were going to Royal 35 Steakhouse to eat. I knew that had to be Charlotte's doing because Celeste didn't normally eat at such fancy places. After dropping the kids off, I decided to go by the restaurant.

After putting on a baseball cap low on my face, I went in. Once I was at the hostess stand, I immediately spotted Celeste, Charlotte, and Laurel. I flashed the hostess a fifty-dollar bill and asked her to seat me near them. He quickly agreed. After I got seated, I ordered something to drink and started listening to their conversation.

"Wait a minute...Miss Goodie Two Shoes finally let a woman go down on her? Welcome to the dark side, bitch," I heard Charlotte's loud ass say.

"I can't believe you had a threesome. How was it?" Laurel asked.

"Better than I ever imagined. I mean, I've watched them on Pornhub for the sex scenes in my books, but actually participating in one is a whole different vibe."

I thought my ears were deceiving me when I heard Celeste

say she had a threesome. When we were younger, I tried to get her to have one with me. Each time, she declined and gave me an excuse. I even offered to let her pick the woman, and she still told me no. To hear that she had one with another man burned me up inside. It took everything in me not to go over there and curse her ass out.

The waitress brought my drink, which I quickly downed, and ordered two more. I sat there and listened as Celeste not only went into detail about the threesome she had, she also stated that she would have another one. I had no idea who this Celeste was. She was not like this when we were married. Whoever this new guy was had turned her into the woman I'd always longed for her to be. It wasn't that Celeste wasn't a good woman; I just wished that she would have opened up and experimented more. Listening to her talk made me wonder if I was the reason she didn't open up. I dismissed the thought and started listening to the conversation again.

"Girl, Kadarius would shit bricks if he knew you had a threesome without him," Laurel told Celeste.

"Man, fuck Kadarius. I still owe him an ass whooping for that shit he pulled at my job!" Charlotte exclaimed.

"What shit he pulled at your job?" Celeste questioned.

"Girl, I forgot to tell you. He brought his punk ass to my job. He tried to make me tell him who you were dating. If I wasn't on the clock, he would have got the business."

"Why didn't you call me?"

"'Cause I didn't need to. I know how to handle his bitch ass."

Celeste went on to tell Charlotte that if I ever bothered her again, to let her know. Charlotte was always running her damn mouth. So far, I still hadn't heard them say anything about the guy Celeste was dating. I was about to give up until Celeste's phone started ringing. She told the ladies it was somebody named Devon.

Bingo! I said to myself.

Just as I was about to pay the bill, Celeste told Charlotte

and Laurel that Devon was about to stop by and meet them. I thought about how lucky my day had gotten. Not only did I find out the name of the guy she was dating, I was about to see him in the flesh. I ordered a meal so that I wouldn't have to worry about the waitress trying to make me leave. Shortly after getting my food, I looked up and saw a guy approaching Celeste's table.

"Hey, Beautiful!" he greeted her.

"Hey there, Handsome. This is my sister, Charlotte and my best friend, Laurel. Ladies, this is Devon."

"Damn, you fine!" Charlotte said.

Her ass had always been the hoe of the group, so her words didn't surprise me. I pulled out my phone to get some pictures of him. I was going to get them to one of the private investigators my firm uses and have them find out who he is. I signaled the waitress and handed her a hundred-dollar bill. I knew that was more than enough to take care of my tab. I went home and hit up the private investigator. He told me to email him the pictures I had of Devon. Pretty soon, I was going to know everything I needed to know about the man who had my wife's attention.

Chapter 21: I Hate the Club

"Come on D, this shit finna be lit," said Sebron, pulling into the huge parking lot of Club Navajo. Today was Serenity's birthday and she paid to rent the entire damn club, which we knew she would. It wouldn't be like Serenity if she didn't go all out.

"I told Ren I ain't felt like coming out. I don't know why her ass went all out renting this club." She could have simply thrown something plain and simple. This shit she had going here was completely out of my comfort zone. I know that is hard to believe since I film porn for a living, but truth be told, I hated the clubs; they were overrated.

"Nigga, you used to love the clubs back in the day."

"That was back then, this is now."

"Damn, you must have finally found a girl."

"What gives you that impression?"

"Your ass used to love the club, now you hate it. And let's not forget that Ren invited you here. There're bottles and bitches up in there. Back then, you wouldn't have passed up a chance to get some of that."

"I just don't feel like the club scene tonight, man," I replied, keeping it short and simple. I didn't want him in my business, and I didn't truly know what Celeste and I had going on. After what happened between her, Ren, and I, I saw a new side of her. It'd been two months since that happened, and we've gone at it three more times. But I called everything quits due to Serenity's growing suspicion. When she noticed that I started giving Celeste more attention during sex, it didn't sit right with her. After I slipped up and told her I loved her while we were fucking, I deaded the entire threesome ordeal. Serenity got in my ass about it, and the last thing I needed was her fucking up what Celeste and I were building. I was more relieved at the fact that when we did fuck, we were all high as fuck off sativa.

Celeste was so stuck on the high from the sativa as well as the high from the sex, she didn't even hear me tell her that I loved her.

.

"Yeah, whatever nigga. That entire attitude gonna change when you bust through the doors. Don't think I don't know how you get when you start feeling a bitch? All I wanna do is meet her."

"There's nobody to meet, Sebron, damn," I laughed.

"Oh, so she not new? Let me find out you and Ren finally got together."

"Man, fuck that. You know I wouldn't cross that line with Ren. She just too wild for me. We're best friends; I'm not over-stepping that boundary."

"Man, put that best friend bullshit in the trash. You know you love Ren."

"Yeah, I do, but not in that way."

"You know that girl like you, though."

"I know, and I deaded that already."

"Whatever, nigga. Sometimes I think you gay. Ren a fine piece of ass, and I don't know if you know, but lil' baby can ride some dick. She a whole pornstar — literally. I think if she wasn't a pornstar, mama would accept a lil' relationship between y'all."

"Man, go somewhere with that bullshit," I replied, poppin' my collar on my black Versace jacket. I sported a pair of black True Religion jeans and a gold, black, and white Versace Barocco Acanthus print silk shirt, which was unbuttoned just enough to show the artwork on my chest. A pair of white Yeezy's clung to my feet while ice dripped around my neck, shining like the sun. I rarely stepped out like that, but when I did, I did.

Since we were already well known, we skipped the entire line and went inside. when we stepped foot through the door, I knew we weren't going to be disappointed. Megan Thee Stallion's latest song, "Sugar Baby", blasted through the club as half naked women threw their asses back like this was their anthem.

"Oh, he want a bad bitch? Well, I want a nigga with some money and a long dick. Buy me everything in my cart if you my boyfriend!" Serenity rapped, coming up to Sebron and me with two other women following her pursuit. One thing Serenity knew how to do was cause a scene with her looks. She sported jet black hair that looked around to be forty inches. She had on an all-white see through jumper with a black G-string, and her breasts was on full display. She had a crown laced with real diamonds on her head with a pair of brand new silver Versace heels I bought her. One thing Serenity wasn't afraid to do was show off her body, and her body was indeed something to look at. This wasn't the first time she came out in public with her ass and titties on full display. She was so decked out, that her nipple rings had real diamonds in them. And whoever did her makeup did one hell of a good ass job because she was looking beautiful. Shit, she had my soldier standing at attention just from looking at her. Ren even had the bottle girls and caterers dressed in skimpy ass shit. They wore white lingerie and tiaras on their heads as well.

"Hey best friend, what do you think?" she smiled, wrapping her arms around me and looking up in my face.

"You really outdid yourself, I tell you that," I replied, looking around at everyone enjoying themselves.

"Thank you, I try. I see our lil' guest didn't get the invitation. It's sad, I wish she would have been here," she whispered in my ear so Sebron couldn't hear.

"Enough of that, she was busy."

"Hm, you would know."

"Damn, best friend, can I get a hug?" said Sebron with open arms and a Cheshire Cat grin spread across his face. Serenity laughed before letting me go and going to hug him. He looked up at me, wiggling his eyebrows as if he done hit the jackpot.

"Girl, I just wanna drank your bath water," said Sebron, eyeing her up and down.

"So does every other man in the room. Sebron, this pussy

would hurt you. Go find somebody to play with," she laughed, letting him out of her embrace. When Sebron saw a group of bad bitches dancing in the middle of the floor, I already knew it was his cue to run off, leaving me and Ren alone.

"We need to talk," she said, grabbing my hand and leading me up to the V.I.P. section that was full of strippers, women kissing on one another, and men getting lap dances. She pushed me down in the velvet chair before sitting in my lap.

"Wassup?" I sighed, hoping she wasn't coming at me with no bullshit. It was already bad enough that I didn't wanna be here. I was only here to make her happy, and I already knew the shit she was about to release from her lips would make me regret coming out.

"Celeste hasn't been answering my calls. You know anything about that?" she asked, licking her plump, thick lips.

"Celeste is her own person. Why you asking me?"

"Because, I tried to call her three days ago to see if she would be down for another lil' night of fun. I would have really enjoyed my birthday some more if we did a lit —."

"Look, I cut all that off."

"What? Why?"

"Ren, you know why. Come on, let's talk about something else. I don't wanna ruin a good night."

"Hpmh, yeah, whatever. Come dance with me then." She smiled and pulled me from my seat. Her soft hands roamed my chest before she licked her lips while dancing on me. After a night full of throwing back drinks, dancing, and being rubbed up on by Ren and a handful of other women who were in the building, I headed back to my place. Serenity even decided to crash over at my place. Thinking that I was gonna call it a night, Serenity was already on top of me, kissing me and peeling off my clothes like it was nothing.

"Come on, Devon, I'm horny," she slurred, trying to reach in my pants and stroke me, but I stopped her. I was tired, and I already had a headache from all that loud ass music bumping in my ear. Any other time, I would have been ready to rearrange everything inside of her, but I was drunk as hell with a killer headache, and the last thing on my mind was pussy.

"Nobody told your ass to get loose with two whole bottles of D'usse. Come on Ren, just sleep it off."

"Come on, just put the tip in."

"No, take your ass to sleep now, come on," I said, trying to push her off of me, but she wouldn't budge.

"Come on, please?" she pleaded, grabbing my hand, placing it on her breast. Already knowing I wasn't gonna hear the end of it, I gave in. I messaged her ass as she sucked and kissed on my neck while stroking my dick through my Calvin Klein boxers.

"Damn," I hissed under my breath.

She took off her jumper and tried to ease down on my dick without a condom. I almost slung her drunk ass to the floor like a wrestler.

"Yo, what you doing?" I asked, holding her waist to stop her.

"What does it look like?"

"You know where the condoms at Ren, stop playing with me."

"Wow," she laughed to herself as she got off of me.

"Wow what? You ain't ever get offended when I corrected you about that shit before. Stop playing with me, Ren. What's going on with you?"

"You love her?" she asked, standing over me in damn near all of her naked glory.

"What?"

"I heard you. You told Celeste that you loved her. The fuck was that about, huh? How long have we known each other? How long have I been feeling you, Devon? I know you meant it; I know how you sound when you mean it. Whenever you're inside of me, you never tell me you fucking love me! You pushed me to the fucking side and fucked her like you had something to prove. You never fuck me the way you fucked her in front of me, and that shit don't sit right with me. The way you touched and kissed her, you were gentle yet understanding with her.You act like your ass almost got stuck in her pussy the way you came. You never cum that hard for me. Why is she so different from me, huh?!"

"Look, you need to chill."

"I don't need to do shit! Do you love her?! Do you fucking love her?!" she yelled in my face, and I could tell by the way her voice cracked, she was about to start crying.

I knew she was gonna bring that shit up. I wasn't sure what the fuck I was thinking in that moment, but all I knew was that I felt like it was only me and Celeste in that moment. I was slowly giving her deep strokes, hitting every spot she never knew she had. And the moment we came at the same time, I got caught up and said those words. I loved her personality and the person she was, but I didn't know what was behind me telling her that. I was high as fuck; that could have played a part in it, but it was evident that I was feeling Celeste. Shit, I could've told her I loved her because her pussy had a nigga feeling like a crack addict.

"Do you fucking love her?" she repeated herself.

"No."

"Quit fucking lying to me!" she yelled.

"Look, I'm finna call you an Uber."

"Call me an Uber?! Like I'm some hoe?! You gonna kick me out and call me a fucking Uber?! I can't believe you. Save your fucking money. I know my way home; just know I ain't taking this shit lying down. This ain't over with, Devon." she said, picking up her clothes and slamming my bathroom door. Her ass had better luck just walking outside butt ass naked because her 'fit was technically that. I ran my hands down my face, trying to figure out what the hell I got myself into.

Chapter 22: How Does It Feel

"Bye babies. I love y'all and please be safe," I said to Cassie and KJ as they went out of the door with my mother, who was in town for the week. She wanted to spend some time with the kids before she went back home. I was more so happy that Cassie was finally back to her old self. I remember when I couldn't get her out of the house at all, but now she was ready to dip and leave the house every ten seconds.

"Mama, please be careful with my babies."

"I got this; you know who you talking to? These my grand-babies; I got this, Celeste."

"I know, it's just that I'm on edge every time they leave my sight," I sighed.

"The recovering phase takes some time, sweetie. Cassie is home safe and so are you. I could only imagine what the sick bastard did to you and my baby girl, Cassie. You are fine, and you will be fine. Right now, you should only be worried about these babies, your career, and yourself. Kadarius's trifling ass is finally out of the picture and you're finally getting back to your old self. You got this, baby girl."

"Come on, Grandma!" yelled KJ, sticking his head out of the window of my mother's cream-colored Escalade.

"That's my cue," laughed my mother.

"See you later, Mama, love you."

"Love you more," she replied as I hugged her then let her go. After watching them pull off, I closed my door and pulled my phone out to see if Devon wanted to come over. I haven't seen him in a minute, and I missed his company. As soon as I was about to press his contact, I heard pounding on my door, making me jump. Since my anxiety was already at an all-time high,

I went to my kitchen and grabbed a butcher knife, easing up on the door.

"Who is it?" I asked.

"Who you think it is? Open the door!" yelled Kadarius, banging on my door like he was the fucking police.

Sighing in relief yet filled with annoyance, I swung my door open to see him fuming.

"The kids already left with my mother, and you already know you have them on the weekends. What are you doing here?" I sighed.

"You know what the fuck I'm doing here," he replied, pushing past me and pacing back and forth like a crackhead.

"What the fuck?! Kadarius, you got five seconds to tell me what the fuck you doing here before I gut your ass like a fucking fish. Now what the fuck are you doing here?"

"So, you just a big ass hoe, huh?! You a dirty fucking hoe, that's exactly what the fuck you are."

"Excuse me?!" I yelled with wide eyes. Who the fuck did this nigga think he was, barging up into the residence I pay bills in and slandering my name?

"You out here fucking judging me for what I did? Yeah, I was fucking wrong! I was wrong, I can admit that, but this new you I'm seeing, I've never seen you in the way that I'm seeing you now. You out here fucking motherfuckers and acting so fucking innocent. You always been a dirty ass hoe, that's probably why Tykell did what the fuck he did. You out here having threesomes with motherfuckers — a motherfucker you don't even fucking know. You probably gave Tykell some pussy back then while you were with me, and now your ass is playing the innocent role. And you fucking Devon James, huh? You're fucking pathetic, I —."

Before he could finish his sentence, I rocked his shit. If my kids weren't on my mind, I would have sliced and diced his ass up like a fucking tomato with this big ass butcher knife in my hand. I wanted to kill his ass, but I knew I would go to jail if I did. I didn't know what the fuck was going on with Kadarius, but one thing he wasn't going to do was jump up in my business and come at me the way he was. I was more so curious on how the fuck he knew I had a threesome. How the fuck did his ass know about Devon? At this point, I was fed up, and I was gonna show him that I was fed up. He wasn't about to come up in my shit and bully me like I was still married to his gay ass. He better had to go find some dick to suck because I wasn't taking his shit. I knelt down to his level while he was still laid out on the floor, trying to figure out what just happened. I pressed the knife to his throat and laughed.

"The next time you waltz your big bodied, gay ass up in my spot thinking you gonna be in my business like a little high school girl, I will fuck you up, and I put that on my babies' heads, nigga. We are not together, we will never be back together, and this is my pussy. I do whatever the fuck I wanna do with it. And, I will fuck who I wanna fuck as long as I'm not fucking you. Do I bust up in your motherfucking place telling you who dick you can suck or who you can't stick your dick in? Listen here, RuPaul, next time you come in my shit, I will fucking butcher your ass. And if you're wondering, yes, I did have a motherfucking threesome, and that shit was spectacular. Get out my motherfucking house," I said, getting up and opening my front door. He looked at me, without even saying anything. He walked out and went to his car that I didn't even know was parked across the street. I watched him speed off, looking mad as hell.

Exactly what the fuck I thought, I said to myself, slamming my house door and going into my kitchen.

"Alexa, call Boo Daddy," I said, laughing at the corny ass name I put in my phone.

"Calling Boo Daddy," said Alexa, making me laugh even more.

"Wassup," he answered.

"Hey, are you busy?" I asked, placing the butcher knife back where it was.

"Nah, I'm just in here watching TV."

"Wanna come over?"

"Come over where?"

"My place, Devon. Where else?" I laughed.

"Oh shit. My bad. Of course, baby girl," he laughed.

"Where the hell else would I tell you to come to?"

"You've never invited me to your place, so I got a lil' stupid for a second."

"You straight. I'll text you my address."

"Alright, see you then."

After texting Devon my address, I straightened up my house to make it seem somewhat presentable. Going to my full body mirror, I shrugged, deciding to keep on what I had on, even though I looked like shit. I can't remember the last time I got excited for a man to come over to my place. Devon made me wanna beat my face and throw on the finest thing in my closet, but I know that wasn't necessary. He told me I looked beautiful regardless of what I wore. But my messy bun, tank top, and cookie monster pajama pants said otherwise. My face was bare, showing every freckle and dark spot. I lit some of my Yankee Candles before actually deciding to change. I threw on my red sundress that I usually wore around the house, and I let my hair down, letting my natural, deep coils fall free. After applying some strawberry sorbet EOS lip balm to my plump, full lips, I went to the kitchen to grab my phone.

It didn't take long before I heard my doorbell ring, and a grin as wide as the ocean formed on my face. Running to the door, I swung it open, revealing Devon, who had a bag of Chinese food in his hands. I licked my lips, eyeing him down as he was dressed down in Nike from head to toe. He had on a navy blue Nike tracksuit with a pair of white Nike Huaraches clinging to his feet. He even had on a white Nike snapback.

"Look like you finna head to the gym ain't it?" I laughed.

"I was just getting out the shower and threw this on."

"Mhm, yeah right."

"For real. And I hope you like Chinese food."

"I do."

"Good, where's the kids?"

"With my mom."

"I know you relieved."

"I am," I laughed, leading him to my kitchen.

"They not that bad."

"Oh, sweetheart, you haven't met that KJ yet."

"Well, one day I'd like too."

"You might."

"You have a beautiful home, by the way."

"Oh, thank you. I just moved here. I still have my other house that's on the other side of town. After everything, I wanted to start fresh."

"What you gonna do with the other house?"

"Sell it or give it to my ex-husband."

"I feel you."

We both grabbed our plates and sat in the living room to watch old movies. We went from *The Five Heartbeats*, *The Temptations*, *Precious*, and *Norbit*, to *What's Love Got to Do With It*. We were currently laid up in my bed, enjoying each other's company and listening to R&B and Soul.

Through drought and famine, natural disasters
My baby has been around for me
Kingdoms have fallen, angels be calling
None of that could ever make me leave
Every time I look into your eyes I see it
You're all I need
Every time I get a bit inside I feel it

Daniel Caesar's song, "Get You", blasted softly through my room. Devon laid between my legs, letting me run my fingers through his waves while his arms were wrapped around my waist.

"Can I ask you something?" he mumbled with his eyes half closed.

"Of course."

"Do you have a problem with me cutting off the threesome shit?"

"No, I don't have a problem. I mean, it was fun of course,

in the beginning when I first did it but it started to become awkward, you know?"

"Awkward how?"

"Devon, sweetheart it seemed like there were times it was just me and you fucking while Serenity watched."

"You got a problem with that?" he asked, looking up at me, showing me his perfect smile.

"You know I don't," I laughed.

"Good. I actually wanted you for myself, if you want me to be real. I got tired of Ren trying to make me share you."

"Well, I've been missing you."

"How much?"

"Shut up and come kiss me and see," I smiled.

He got up and pulled his white tee over his head before getting in between my legs and kissing me. The scent of his Dior cologne filled my lungs like it was nothing. His lips moved from my lips to my neck, knowing it was my spot. I became wet just from his touch. He came out of his sweatpants before kissing me all over.

"Can I ask you something?" he asked.

"Yeah."

"Be my girl?"

"What?"

"You heard me. Look, Celeste. I don't know if I'm moving too fast or what, but I'm feeling you and I can't get you out of my head sometimes. You're different, and that's something I like. I've never been so drawn to a woman a day in my life, and it's like, you're everything I want a woman. I know you just getting out of a marriage and you got your kids and everything to think about but, I just wanted to ask you before it was too late."

"Yeah."

"Yeah, like you agree or.."

"Yeah, I'll be your girl," I laughed, watching his face light up like the sun.

"Well, I'm about to tear this shit up. You done made my day," he laughed, coming out of his boxers and sliding my dress up. He pulled my panties off before poking at my entrance, sliding in slowly. I bit my lip, hissed in pain, and tried to get accustomed to his size. This man was blessed, and if he fucked a bitch the right way with what was in between his legs, you would have had to put a bitch on suicide watch.

And when we're making love
Your cries they can be heard from far and wide
It's only the two of us
Everything I need's between those thighs
Every time I look into your eyes I see it
You're all I need
Every time I get a bit inside I feel it

Devon had me in here screaming so loud in pleasure that I was shocked the neighbors didn't call the police. Shit, by the end of this, they would probably know his name.

"Fuck, you so tight," he groaned, pinning my leg on his shoulder and easing in and out of my treasure. He made me look down to see my juices coating his dick.

Wrapping both of my legs around his waist, he placed his hand above me using the headboard as support, as he delivered long deep strokes my way.

"Fuck, Devon!" I yelled as he hit another spot that drove my body crazy.

"Take that shit. This your dick, baby," he whispered in my ear, making the hairs on the back of my neck stand up. And just like that, I came all over his dick. It was like this nigga was the Energizer Bunny because even though I busted my nut, he kept on going. When I saw that look in his eyes, I knew he was about to cum right after.

"I'm about to cum," he moaned in my ear.

"Cum for me, baby," I whispered in his ear while licking, kissing, and sucking on his neck.

"Fuck, girl, I love you," he groaned, letting a full load go. My legs were shaking, and my mind was going in circles from him telling me that he loved me. He looked at me, trying to figure out how to explain himself. Before he could say anything, I grabbed his face and pecked his lips.

"I love you too."

Chapter 23: When Secrets Come to Light

I had been on cloud nine since the day Devon and I made our relationship official. There was a part of me that was nervous. I was with Kadarius for so long that I wasn't sure if I knew how to be with another man. I called Charlotte and expressed my concerns to her. She assured me that Devon was nothing like Kadarius and that I would be fine. She was right. I had to let go of the bullshit and move forward.

Speaking of Kadarius, he called me earlier and asked me to meet him at our old house. I originally told him no, but he said it was important, so I went.

"What's so important that I had to meet you over here?" I asked with an attitude when I got there.

"Well, hello to you too, Celeste," Kadarius replied.

"Cut the bullshit. This isn't a social visit. Now tell me what you want so I can get the hell out of here."

"Fine...I'm here to give you an ultimatum."

"An ultimatum? The fuck?"

"Yes. You either stop seeing the Devon guy or I will take you to court and get custody of the kids."

I laughed so hard; I made my stomach hurt. He is a lawyer, so I know he knows damn well that in order for kids to be taken away from their mother, the father has to show that she is unfit. That was something I most certainly was not.

"Kadarius, stop wasting my time. We both know you wouldn't win. What would you tell the judge? You don't like my boyfriend?"

"I would tell them that you are being reckless. Having threesomes isn't a good look, my dear."

"A threesome, huh? That's all you got? Go ahead. Take me

to court and embarrass yourself," I told him as I turned to walk away.

"They might not say anything about a threesome, but they will defintely say something about a murder."

I stopped in my tracks when he said that. If he was talking about Tykell, he was going to have to come better than that. We both knew that mystery woman killed Tykell. Before I could say anything, he continued.

"You see, when Cassie went missing, I thought it was Reggie who took her. I confronted him, things got out of hand, and I killed him."

"Okay, you killed him. What does that have to do with me?"

"Nothing right now. However, if the police were to get an anonymous tip that his body is buried in this yard..."

I stood there speechless. There was no way in hell a body was buried in my yard. There was just no way. Rather than say anything, I jumped in my car and sped away. I went to Charlotte's house. Thankfully, she was home.

"What's wrong? Whose ass I need to beat?" she asked when she opened the door and saw the look on my face.

"Kadarius is trying to frame me for murder."

"He what? Explain!"

I told her the conversation I had with Kadarius. By the time I was done, she was pacing her living room floor. She was livid.

"He has to be lying! Even if he did kill him, why bury him in the backyard of your house?"

"I have no idea. What if he isn't lying, though? He's a lawyer. He can easily manipulate the system. Oh, my God. I'm going to prison."

"Calm down! You are not going to prison, you hear me? Not on my watch. The first thing we gotta do is find out if that body is really there. You're staying here with me for the rest of the day. I don't trust that bitch nigga, Kadarius."

"I was supposed to hang out with Devon."

"Have him come here."

I called Devon and told him we were going to hang out at Charlotte's house for the day, and he was fine with it. My nerves were shot and I'm sure they would be for the rest of the day. Reggie's disappearance was all over the news when it first happened. Due to the bullshit he had put my family through, I didn't give a damn. It never dawned on me to question Kadarius. Besides, I was busy trying to get my daughter home. Things were just now starting to go good in my life, and now this shit.

Chapter 24: My Sanity

It's been two weeks since I threatened Celeste. I was a very reasonable and persistent man. All I wanted was for my family to get back together. At night, I drove myself crazy trying to figure out why I led into temptation and ruined a good thing. It was as if my heart and my mind were at a constant game of tug a war. Part of me blamed myself, part of me blamed Reggie, I then blamed Tykell, and then most of my blame went to Celeste. Growing up, I was taught to fight for what I wanted, and if I wanted it bad, I was taught to get it by any means necessary. I found joy in seeing Celeste sweat like a dog in heat. I knew her better than anybody else, and if she got curious enough, she was gonna go and poke the cat.

When I saw her still messing around with that Devon nigga, it had my blood boiling like the sun. I decided to show her better than I could tell her on how good I was on my word. I sat across the street from my house, waiting for my plan to fall into action. I was a lawyer long enough to know how to properly set someone up. The same shovel that I buried Reggie with was the same shovel I took to Celeste's new place. She recently used it in her garden, and it was nothing to sneak back into her spot and switch the shovel back out. I found one of the lonely crackheads on the street and paid them to do the dirty work. It costed me nothing but twenty dollars and a forty to get them to agree to it. I gave them a burner phone and a message, knowing for sure that Celeste was gonna be here in no time.

I didn't usually drag my kids into my antics, but I knew how much she loved them. After getting a call saying that KJ was dropped off at the old house after school, I knew she would be here in seconds. After what happened to Cassie, she didn't let the kids out of her sight for nothing. Hearing that KJ was at the old house by himself would have triggered her. When I saw her car pull into the driveway hectically, a grin spread across my face. When I saw her trying to get into the house, I shook my head at how well this was going. I had someone change the locks to the house for me so her keys wouldn't work. I saw her banging on the door, yelling for KJ to open it. I guess she grew tired of banging because she went around the house, exactly where I wanted her. I even dug up the body and had Reggie laid out in the open.

It wasn't even a whole ten seconds before I phoned my homeboy, who worked at the police station. They came in deep with their sirens blaring. When I heard Celeste's blood curdling scream, I slouched down in my seat and watched the cops kick the door open as they went through the house in just the knick of time. I watched as they brought her out in handcuffs. Tears streamed down her face while she tried to explain her innocence. After seeing them haul her high and mighty ass to jail, I drove off back to my place where the kids were. When I got there, my mother already had them washed up and ready to go back to Celeste. I knew she was gonna try and pull this shit. Every time I tried to steal an extra day with my kids, my mother wasted no time coming in and hauling them back to Celeste.

"Hey Ma, I thought I told you they were staying with me for an extra day."

"You know that's not what you and Celeste agreed to. I'm trying to keep the friction at a bare minimum between you two."

"Ma, these are my kids, not yours. KJ, Cassie, go to your room so I can talk to Grandma," I said. They looked at me hesitantly before doing as told.

"Excuse me?" said my mother.

"Ma, I didn't mean it like that."

"Then what did you mean it like, Kadarius? Look, we need to talk anyway."

"Talk about what?"

"About you. I'm worried about you, sweetheart."

"Didn't seem pretty worried when Celeste divorced me."

"Look, you're a grown man, and I've always raised you to do what you believe and what you love. But you cheated on that woman with a man — a man, Kadarius. That is the biggest betrayal a wife can never come back from. You hurt her, and most importantly, you hurt your kids."

"I'm not in the mood to argue."

"I never said you had to argue with me; we're talking like two adults. Celeste is a good woman, and she didn't deserve that. The kids have even said you've been acting differently. What's going on with you?"

"You think she's so innocent, huh?"

"Because she is," she replied, looking at me as if she wanted to put hands on me for questioning her.

"I've been tryna keep this on the low because of the kids and because I still love her. But do you wanna know why I'm not with the man I cheated on her with? Because she killed him."

"What?" she gasped.

"She killed him, Ma. She killed him." I fake cried, falling into her arms. One thing I knew how to do was play the part, and confiding in my mother about Celeste's alleged murder was perfect. My mother rubbed circles in my back, comforting me At one point, I couldn't tell if my tears were real or fake. The truth was, I really did miss Reggie. Even though he annoyed the fuck out of me, I missed him. He was my go-to man when I couldn't talk to Celeste about certain shit, and that's what made me more attracted to him.

"It's okay, baby. How long have you known this?" she asked.

"It's been a while now, Ma. As soon as she found out about him, she stalked him and killed him."

"How did you know? Did you see it?"

"Yes, I saw the body and everything. I watched her bury him in our old backyard."

"Look, I think we should keep this information to ourselves right now."

"What?" I replied, looking at her like she was crazy. My

mother loved Celeste as if she was her own daughter. One thing she wouldn't do was snitch on her. I guess I had to up my game some more to make my mother turn on her.

"You heard me. Look, we can meet with Celeste and talk to her."

"Ma, no. That's not the only fucked up thing she did. She's a fucked up individual. After she got kidnapped, she went through a lot. When she came back, she wasn't the same. She beats the kids, and that's why I try to keep them over here as much as possible."

"What? Kadarius, are you serious?" my mother quizzed, looking at me in shock.

"Yes."

"Why? When? What the hell? When the hell were you going to tell me about this?"

"I couldn't. I told you, I still love her, but she doesn't love me anymore, Ma. I tried to reason with her. I even threatened to go to the cops, and she laughed in my face. She said she would send me to jail and keep the kids away from me. I can't lose my kids, Ma. I love my kids." I broke down again.

She held me tight before letting out a deep sigh.

"We're going to the police station right now."

"What?"

"Right now, let's go. I'm taking the kids to your father."

I watched as my mother grabbed her purse, fuming, raging with anger. At times, I questioned my sanity while coming up with this. But my sanity had nothing to do with my heart and how hard I fought to protect it. She wanted to see the bad guy in me; I was gonna show her the bad guy.

Chapter 25: Lies on Top of Lies

Ring...ring...ring

I looked at my phone and saw that an unknown number was calling me. I usually didn't answer them, but since I hadn't been able to get in touch with Celly in the last few hours, I decided to.

"Hello!"

"You have a collect call from Celeste, an inmate at a county jail. Press one to accept the charges."

I immediately pressed one. There were all kind of things going through my head. *Why the hell was my sister in jail?*

"Char!" Celeste screamed.

"Celeste why the hell are you in jail?"

"I need you to come bail me out. I'll explain when you get here. I got some money stashed at my house. Not sure if that's enough. I'll pay you back. Oh, and can you call Devon for me? I put his number in your phone the night you met him."

"Don't worry about paying me back. You're my sister. I'm about to call Devon, and we will be on the way to get you. Where are the kids?"

"With Kadarius's mom."

The way she said that let me know that his bitch ass had something to do with the situation. I made a mental note to get my Glock out of my safe. I knew I was going to have to shoot that nigga one day. After hanging up with Celeste, I called Devon.

"Hello," he answered on the second ring.

"Hey, Devon. This is Charlotte, Celeste's sister."

"Thank goodness you called me. I was looking for you on social media. Have you heard from Celeste? We were supposed to meet up last night, but she's not answering her phone. I'm getting worried."

"That's why I'm calling. Celeste just called me from jail. She didn't say why she's locked up, but I'm sure it has something to do with that bitch ass ex-husband of hers. Anyway, meet me at the county so we can get her out of there."

"I have some money in my stash. I'll help get her out. See you there."

That gesture alone let me know Devon was a much better man that Kadarius's bitch ass. I went to my safe and pulled out fifty thousand dollars. I was so distracted by the fact that she was in jail, I didn't think to ask how much her bail was. Hopefully between the money I had and the money Devon was bringing, it would be enough.

It took me forty-five minutes to get to the county jail because of traffic. Once I got there, Devon was already inside. Before I could speak to him, he blurted out what he found out so far.

"They picked her up for murder! Who the hell would Celeste murder?"

"Murder? Ain't no way. That's got to be a mistake."

"I called a lawyer friend of mine and had him meet me down here. He's getting her out now. Apparently, the only reason she got bail is because they have no physical evidence. They received a tip."

None of the shit Devon was telling me made sense. Who the hell would say my sister murdered somebody? I couldn't wait until she got out so I could talk to her. I paced back and forth in the hall as I waited on them to let Celeste go.

"Everything is going to be ok, Charlotte. I know you just met me, but I love your sister. I will body anybody who brings harm her way."

"I believe you. The fact that you beat me down here and came with a lawyer lets me know everything I need to know."

He hugged me and we continued to wait. An hour later, Celeste was coming out. I immediately noticed how puffy her eyes were. That let me know she had been crying for a while. Shit made my blood boil.

"Celly! Are you okay? Did they hurt you?"

"Physically, I'm okay. Mentally, not good. Can you take me to a hotel so I can shower? I'll explain everything after that."

"A hotel? Why can't you go to my place or Charlotte's?" Devon asked.

"It's not safe."

"Not safe? What the hell? You know what? Okay. We'll take you to a hotel. Let's go."

We all got in my car, and I drove to the InterContinental in Times Square. Celeste swore she didn't need anything fancy, but after the shit she had gone through, she deserved it. I booked a two-bedroom Manhattan Suite because I was certain after hearing what happened to her, Devon and I would be staying with her. I got it for a week. There was a gift shop downstairs. Devon bought her some outfits.

Once we were in the room, Celeste went to shower. Devon ordered lunch for us. When she got out, we sat in silence, waiting for the food. Ten minutes later, it came. Once we all had our plates fixed, I started grilling Celeste.

"Now, how the hell did you end up in jail for murder?" I asked her.

"Kadarius is framing me for the murder of Reggie."

"Who is Reggie?" Devon asked.

"His boyfriend?" I asked.

"Yes, Char, his boyfriend. Remember we thought he was the one who kidnapped Cassie? Well, Kadarius killed him and buried him in the backyard of our house. I thought something was going on with KJ and when I showed up at the house, I saw his body there. Before I could even do anything, the police showed up and booked me."

"Why the hell would he frame you, though? This isn't making sense," Devon questioned.

"He came to me a few days ago and told me if I didn't take him back, he would tell the police I killed Reggie."

"That son of a bitch! Why didn't you say anything? We

could have dealt with this before it got too far," I asked her.

"I honestly didn't take him seriously. Oh! I didn't tell you the worst part. His mother has filed child abuse charges against me. She's claiming that I beat Cassie and KJ. They are in Kadarius's custody until an investigation is complete. So, not only do I have a murder trial to get ready for, I can't even talk to nor see my children," Celeste cried.

"It's okay, baby. Don't cry. I promise you, that nigga gonna get his."

"He damn sure is. Do you have any proof that he and Reggie were messing around? What about an alibi for the night Reggie was supposedly murdered?"

"There is a tape of them having sex in the trunk of my car under my spare tire."

"That would work against you. He could say you killed Reggie out of spite, "Devon told me.

"Well, my alibi should get me off. If he was killed the day Cassie went missing, I was at the police station most of the day. When I wasn't at the station, there was an officer with me out looking for her. I don't even know how it ended up at my house."

"His ass put it there! Kadarius think he slick, but he fucking with the wrong one. I will bury his ass. Here's what we are going to do. We're going to stay here until after this mess is over. I'll go over to your house to get clothes and see if I can find out how that shovel got there."

"Check my cameras. I tried to tell that cop that, but he wouldn't listen."

"I'll have your lawyer bring that up. Char, I'm going to have him get an officer to escort you to her house. We don't need anybody saying the evidence was tampered with."

"That's fine. After that, I'm getting my gun, and I'm going to visit Mr. Kadarius. He got me fucked up if he thinks I'm about to let this ride."

"Charlotte, no! I've already lost my kids. I can't lose you too," Celeste cried.

I lied and told her I would let it go. There was no way he

was about to get away with this shit. That ass was mine.

Chapter 26: Actions and Consequences

Celeste

Six Months Later

It'd been six months since the entire ordeal, and everything was slowly getting figured out. The kids were back in my custody, and Kadarius was now under investigation after everything was presented to the court. Part of me was happy for things to be slowly returning to how they were, but all I could do was sit back and think about how Kadarius flipped the way he did. I was stuck in between a rock and a hard place because I never thought he would go this hard to manipulate me into getting back with him. He knew what I went through with Tykell, and for him to turn around and pull the shit Tykell pulled really fucked with my head.

It was twelve in the morning, and I was up sitting in bed thinking about some heavy shit. I fought so hard to get my head back in the game, but I was sinking fast and I hated it. I hated that I was giving Kadarius the satisfaction. You would have thought that I would have had some type of satisfaction from him going to jail, but I didn't.. Kadarius being gay and cheating on me with a man was my breaking point. Was I even meant to be in a relationship? Was I even meant to be loved? Was Devon just like them? Was I just seeing the facade he was wearing when we were together? I didn't wanna think bad about Devon because he had been nothing but good to me, but I couldn't do anything but think about how the last two men I've had relations with were delusional.

"You straight?" asked Devon, emerging from my bathroom, wearing nothing but a pair of Tommy Hilfiger briefs.

"I'm fine," I lied, putting on a fake smile.

"Really?"

"Yeah."

"No, you're not. Talk to me," he said, coming over and getting under the covers, pulling me into his arms.

"I'm scared."

"Scared? Of what?"

"Of the future, Devon. Of not knowing the unknown."

"Baby, everybody's scared of that."

"No, it's just that I've been getting hit by rocks from left to right, and I'm nervous. I recently got the kids back and Kadarius is taken care of already, but I just feel like I'm going back into that place I don't wanna be in."

"You're not going back in that place, especially with me here to help you. You got this, baby."

"I know," I sighed.

"Then act like it."

"I'm trying."

"Hey, I got something that's gonna brighten your mood, though."

"And that is?"

"I wanna introduce you to my family."

"What?"

"Yeah, I wanted to see how you felt about that first. What do you think?"

"Your family? Devon, are you sure?"

"I'm positive. Why wouldn't I be?"

"It just caught me off guard."

"If you're not comfortable meeting them right now, you don't have to."

"No, I'd love to meet them," I smiled.

"I gotta give you a warning; my family can be something else," I laughed.

"Oh, lord."

"Yeah, I —."

His sentence was cut short by his phone going off. He sighed before declining the call. When I saw the hindered look on his face, it concerned me. I've noticed lately that he'd been declining his calls from left to right. Whoever it was, was giving him hell, and he looked infuriated by it.

"You okay?" I asked, grabbing his chin, making him look at me.

"I'm fine."

"Don't pull one of my numbers. Who was that?"

"Ren."

"Ren? Why are you ignoring her?"

"Long story."

"I got time." I smiled and sat up like a big kid with my elbows on my knees, resting my head on my hands.

"She's pissed at me."

"I thought the both of you were best friends."

"We were."

"Uh oh, were? Past tense. What happened?"

"I've told you about how Ren and I go way back. We been tight forever, and I love that girl. I'm not gonna front with you. The last thing I wanna do is start lying in our relationship. Way before the threesome, Ren and I had been fucking around. We were trying out the friends with benefits shit. I never caught feelings for her because I was well aware of our agreement, and I thought she was too, but apparently not. The more we fucked around, the more she started feelin' a nigga."

"Wow," I said, shaking my head. Serenity seemed like the type of girl who didn't take rejection well. Shit, I'd personally seen that she didn't take rejection well.

"That's not even the end of it. For her birthday, I showed up with good intentions. I don't even really fuck with the club scene, but I showed up just to make her happy. I knew she was drunk as hell. And I had a few drinks in my system too, but she was trippin'. We got to my spot, and she feeling up on me and shit. The next thing I knew, she was tryna fuck me without a rubber. Ren never wears protection with the niggas she with in her videos. She wanted me to hit it raw, and I wasn't doing that; I couldn't do that. She started yelling at me and shit about you."

"About me? What about me?"

"When I told you that I loved you, she was pissed. And when Ren gets pissed, she does stupid shit. I haven't really talked to her since that night."

"Wow, so what are you gonna do?"

"Have a talk with her. But I'm with you. You comfortable with Ren still being around?"

"I've never been the type of woman to tell my man who he can and can't hang with. Devon, baby, you're a grown ass man, and you know that me and you are together. If you wanna be friends with Serenity still, do that. If you don't, then don't. But if you do, make sure she knows her boundaries."

"The three of us can talk after we leave from meeting my parents tomorrow."

"Three of us?"

"Yes, the three of us."

"I think this is between just the two of you."

"Nah, you in on this too," he laughed lightly.

"Whatever. You better be glad I love you."

"I love you too," he smiled, pulling me into his arms and kissing me.

I fell asleep in his arms, feeling a sense of security.

Chapter 27: I'll Take Care of You

"My baby must have been hiding you. You're so beautiful." My mother complimented Celeste, making her blush.

I thought it was finally time for her to meet my parent's and I knew my parent's were eager to meet her. After Celeste and I made it official she was all I talked about.

"Oh thank you." Celeste smiled.

"How many children do you have?" my mother asked her, making me give her the side eye.

"Ma." I warned.

"No, it's fine. I have a boy and a girl."

"How precious. So about giving me a grandchild from Devon."

"Ma, chill."

"What? I was just asking."

"So Celeste, I've read some of your books, your talented." Said my sister, changing the subject.

"Oh wow, thank you, I really appreciate that."

"You write books?" my father asked her.

"Yes sir, I do."

"I have to check out some of your work young lady

"I'd love that."

My father looked at me before giving me a smirk. I conversed with my father multiple times about what I wanted in a woman and everything that was being portrayed here today showed that Celeste was just that. They were a little iffy on her having kids but growing up they were always accepting people. They bombarded Celeste with questions for days and I could do nothing but sit back and smile at how excited she was to be around them.

We spent almost the entire day with my family. Shit, everything went too well if you asked me. They were already tryna get me to put a ring on her finger and put a baby in her. My mother, mainly, was ecstatic and I was happy that she could see me happy with someone. They were even trying to take Celeste off of my hands for the rest of the day, but I wasn't comfortable with leaving her alone with them just yet. I had originally planned to just have lunch with my family and introduce them to Celeste, but lunch soon turned into dinner, along with going to an amusement park.

"If you let me, here's what I'll do. I'll take care of you!" Celeste sang loudly to Drake's "Take Care" as we made our way to my apartment.

Ever since we got back into my car, Celeste had been making fun of the nicknames and stories she'd heard from my family ever since we'd gotten back into my car. I couldn't be mad at her. Shit, I sat back and laughed with her. Just sitting in the car and watching her sing and dance in her seat put a smile on my face. She may not have realized how big of an impact she had on me, but it was monumental.

"You still happy I see," I smiled, pulling into the parking lot.

"Of course. You and your family made my day. Why wouldn't I be happy?"

"I'm just skeptical."

"Skeptical about what?"

"How this is gonna turn out. Ren is already up there, and I just don't want shit to get out of hand. I know her, and I know how she can get."

"Hey, we got this. She can't be that bad."

"You have no idea how bad she can be."

"Well, I doubt that it's anything I can't handle."

Deciding to not go back and forth, I got out and opened the door for her. We walked hand in hand upstairs until we got to my apartment. When we got there, the front door was already unlocked. Going inside, Serenity was standing in the middle of the floor with her arms crossed. I already knew from her demeanor and outfit, she came here with impure intentions. She had on a pair of sheer black pants, a black bra, a pair of gold Gucci heels, and her hair was pulled back into a ponytail, showcasing her full facial features.

"I thought you were coming alone." She fake smiled through gritted teeth.

"Nah, I wasn't."

"What is she doing here?" she asked, looking at Celeste as if she was foreign.

"I'm here to talk," said Celeste.

"Well, I'm here to talk with Devon and Devon only."

"Well, whatever you gotta say to Devon, you can say to me," Celeste replied before I could say anything.

"Oh really?" she laughed, walking closer to us, slowly clapping.

"Yes, really," said Celeste, stepping up to her.

I'd never really seen her get like this, so her behavior was catching me completely off guard. I always saw the vulnerable Celeste; I'd never seen her get to this level. I stepped in between the two before turning to Serenity.

"What's this, Devon?" asked Serenity.

"You know what this is."

"You're here to rub your little girlfriend in my face, huh? You know what? I don't give a fuck that she's right here because I'm gonna say what I was gonna say in the beginning. She doesn't fucking deserve you; I do! I'm the one woman who has been by your side since day one, and you push me to the fucking side for some bitch who barely knows you?! She doesn't know the real you, Devon. I do! I love you! She doesn't fucking love you. She's just like the *others* who broke your fucking heart! She doesn't know the real you. I do," Serenity yelled, hitting me in my chest. Part of me felt sorry for her, but the other part of me couldn't feel as bad as I wanted to feel.

I never gave her an impression that we would be together. She knew we wouldn't be together. I couldn't stress that enough, and she knew that. Ren just wanted to make shit complicated. I knew her so well that she didn't even know herself as well as I did. I knew she was going to pull this shit, but little did she know, it wasn't going to work. Ren loved to guilt trip me into shit, and her manipulation tactics weren't about to get me — especially in this situation. I didn't even really know how to respond to her without hurting her feelings, so Celeste stood in front of me and took over.

"Hey, Serenity, I understand your frustrations. Love is a powerful thing, and I know it's hard to back away from someone you love. I know that you and Devon are close, and I would never make you guys end your friendship over me. But the situationship that the both of you had is done. No more sleeping together, no more of what the both of you were doing. Devon and I are together now, and I would like for the both of you to continue to be friends, but you have to respect our relationship. Serenity, you're a cool female, and I like you, but you can get a tad bit out of control sometimes. I just wanted to get a clear understanding that things are going to be cordial."

"Fuck you," she spat, eyeing Celeste up and down as if she wanted to fight her. Celeste looked down and laughed quietly to herself as if she was about to blow.

"You know what, Serenity? You're really a sad case. Here I was coming here with pure intentions, and you're not mature enough to have a grown up conversation."

"Girl, please. Go to hell and burn slowly. You think you're so innocent, huh? You think you're better than me?"

"I never said I was."

"You're right, because you're not. At least I'm not damaged goods. I bet homeboy had a good ol' time with you. Probably did the same to your daught —."

Before I could step in and check her about what she was about to say, Celeste grabbed her by her hair and dragged her across the floor, beating her face in.

"Bitch, if you ever try me again, I'm gonna fuck you up!" she screamed in her face in between punches. For somebody as short as Celeste, she was giving Serenity's ass, who was thicker and a couple of inches taller than her, a run for her money. When I noticed Celeste grab a glass vase to bash it across her head, I rushed over and carried her out of the apartment, kicking and screaming.

"I will kill that bitch! Devon, I put that shit on my kids; I will murder that bitch!" she screamed, trying to break loose.

After I got her calm, I made her drive off to calm down. Serenity and I needed to have a much-needed talk. I went back upstairs to see Serenity coming out of my apartment with a knife, looking around the corners. Celeste's lil' ass really did a number on her because her titties were out, her hair was all over the place, and her pants had a few holes in them from being dragged. When I noticed the knife in her hand and the rage in her eyes, I quickly rushed her back into the apartment before she could get to Celeste.

"Are you fucking crazy?!" I yelled, trying to take the knife away from her, but she kept trying to move it out of my reach.

"You really protecting that bitch?! You let her put her fucking hands on me!" she yelled.

"Ren, stop it! You're out of line."

"Out of line?"

"You were wrong."

"Fuck you! How could you do this to me?!"

"Ren! Stop it! We're nothing! After that shit you pulled, we're through! You know I've been looking hard for someone to love me and be the woman I need. And you tried to fucking run her away on multiple occasions. We're not friends, we're not fucking, we're not nothing. We're done, Ren," I said, shaking my head.

"I'm the woman you need!"

"You're delusional."

"If I can't have you, neither can she," she replied, trying to walk away but I grabbed her to take the knife from her hands. In the midst of struggling to get the knife, we both fell on the floor, and I looked down to see that the knife had plunged deeply into her side.

Chapter 28: Even When Guilty

Kadarius

I sat in the dirty, cold room of the Motel 6, feeling as if I was losing my mind. After everyone found out the truth about me, I was now wanted. I've I'd been on the run for two weeks now, and my face was still plastered all over the news. I was running myself ragged, running myself into a grave. The entire time, I was stuck to think about the consequences of my actions. I was stuck thinking of my life and how I fucked it up with just the snap of a finger. I couldn't believe I was down this low. I was broke, lonely, and most of all, I was scared. Lately, fear had been finding me and beating me down like a slave. It was never like me to have this much fear in my body. I didn't know if it was the drugs and alcohol taking over my mind, or if it was the fear and anxiety drowning me.

I never knew how bad shit was going to get until I experienced it firsthand. Why the fuck did I have to be so curious? Why the hell did I have to step out on my wife for a night of fun? If only I would have known that night of fun would have ruined my life the way it did. My emotions were so fucked up right now, I didn't know how to feel. I missed Reggie like hell because he knew how to sooth my mind during times like this. I missed Celeste because she always gave me the reassurance I needed to hear every morning, noon, and night. Shit, I missed my kids. I missed my old life, and it was killing me every minute, every second.

I never knew I would end up being down this bad. The more time I stayed isolated and, on the run, the more shit sank in and made me feel like less of a man. I literally left the one woman who would go through hell and high water for me for a man who fulfilled my sexual needs. I fought so hard to get her back for various reasons. I didn't wanna see another man do things that I should have been doing to her. I didn't want another man taking in all the glory and love that she had to give. I knew how much of a good woman Celeste was, and I didn't want another man to experience what was, in my mind, still mine.

I reached around to the nightstand and picked up the broken piece of glass that held a line of coke on it. It seemed as if this had been my only getaway now. Placing my finger over one nostril, I placed the other at the end of the line and took it in, feeling that fast paced high settle in like a storm in the Atlantic. I laid back, looking at the dirty ceiling that had mold in certain spots, letting my body slip into a temporary coma. My heart began to beat fast as I took a deep breath.

"Surprised to see you doing that shit."

Looking up, I knew I was losing my mind. Reggie was standing right there, leaning on the wall looking at me with a look of disgust.

"You're not real."

"You want me to be." He smirked deviously, trotting over to me.

"Why are you here?" I asked, looking at the ceiling for a split second before closing my eyes tightly, trying to make it go away.

"Why are you here?"

"Get out of my head."

"How did you feel after you killed me?"

"I'm sorry," I apologized, not knowing if the hallucinations were from the constant drug use, or if Reggie's ghost had come back to haunt me for what I did.

"Fuck your sorry. I loved you, Kadarius. I fucking loved you! And you killed me over a simple misunderstanding! Don't close your fucking eyes; look at me! Look me in my face and tell me why! You killed me for her! For the same bitch who doesn't even want you! Answer me!"

"Get out of my fucking head!" I screamed, getting up and throwing things all over the place.

I yanked the lamp from out of the wall before throwing it across the room. I pulled everything off of the dingy queen-sized mattress. I was going insane. Once I calmed my nerves, I found myself sitting in the corner of the room I destroyed. My knees were tucked in my chest as I cried silently, feeling lost. What the hell was I going to do? I was a lawyer; I knew how this criminology shit went. Was turning myself in really a good idea? Would turning myself in prove to Celeste that I was a changed man? I was doing all of this for her, and it killed me that she didn't notice. Celeste may have thought I was going crazy, but didn't she know that she was the reason I was going crazy?She was the fucking reason I was out of my mind. I had love for her. Celeste's mind, body, and soul made me lust over her like a dog in heat. I guess after losing her, I realized how infatuated I was with her.

All my life, I lived trying to prove myself to people. I tried proving myself to my parents, my coaches, my teammates, and my colleagues. It was all just a waste of time. The person who stuck by my side through everything was the same person I didn't prove shit to, and it showed. Celeste broke her back for me to make sure our family was good, and I fucked it up. My mind was filled with rage, regret, and thoughts so horrendous that it would make the Devil shed a tear. Celeste had already been through way too much with Tykell's crazy ass, and I didn't wanna put her through the same pain he did. I should have been there to protect her, and I was too fucking sidetracked with shit that should have been irrelevant to me.

Many malicious thoughts ran through my head as I took the bottle of Tequila to the head. Should I just kill her new nigga and run off with her to show her how much of a mistake she was making by moving on? Should I just kill us both so no one else could have her? Maybe if I took the kids for ransom, she would sit and hear me out. Downing the rest of the liquor in the bottle, I threw it to the wall, watching it shatter before letting out a gut-wrenching scream. I was losing my mind.

Chapter 29: Mistakes

I had been looking at Ren's body for the last ten minutes or so, and the reality of what I had done still hadn't sunk in. All I wanted to do was have a civil conversation with Ren, but as usual, she went off the deep end. Shit was never supposed to get this far. Tears began to fall from my eyes as I thought about the fact that not only was my best friend dead, but I'm the one who killed her.

"Baby, what's takin' you so....OMG! Devon, what happened? Is she dead?" Celeste asked me.

"It was an accident, I swear. She attacked me and we started tussling. Man, I swear it was an accident. FUCK! I can't go to jail, man. I can't."

"Devon, look at me! Calm down. You are not going to jail. We're going to fix this," she told me while pulling out her phone.

"Who are you calling?"

"Charlotte."

I asked her why she was calling her sister, and she explained that Charlotte knew people who could help us. After she told me that her sister would be here soon, we went and sat in the car. I was shaking the entire time we waited. Celeste kept trying her best to get me to calm down, but nothing worked. I just wanted this nightmare to be over with. About an hour later, Charlotte pulled up. I noticed that a white van pulled up behind her. Two big muscular dudes got out.

"Where is she?" Charlotte asked us.

We, with the big dudes in tow, went back inside where Ren's body was. After they looked to make sure Ren was actually dead, they went out to their van to get some stuff. When they came back inside, they had bleach, trash bags, gloves, and a body bag.

"What in the John Wick type shit is this?" I asked.

Charlotte and Celeste both laughed before telling me to come outside with them. When we got out there, Charlotte told me about the guys.

"They work for this dude I mess with from time to time. He is into some shit that isn't exactly legal, so he keeps a clean-up crew. When Celly called me, I hit him up and told him I needed help. They are very discreet, and nothing will be able to be traced back to you. When you get home, I need you to take off your clothes and get rid of them. I don't mean throw them in the trash either. Better yet, do you have an extra set of clothes in your car?"

I opened the trunk and found a bag that had a pair of shorts and a shirt in it. Since I started staying at Celeste's house from time to time, I always kept clothes in the trunk. I got in my back seat and changed. When I was done, Charlotte told me to leave them on the ground so her guys could pick them up when they were done inside.

I was thankful that Charlotte was there to help, but the shit had my mind wondering. I thought about the murder that Celeste was being framed for and wondered if she did it. I mean, I know she had evidence that proved that her ex-husband did it, however, I wondered if she could have set him up. It wasn't something I was going to bring up to her, though. In fact, after today, I was going to do my best to never piss her off. My ass was not about to end up in the back of a white van.

I'm not sure how much time passed before the guys came out with Ren's body. Seeing the body bag had me in my feelings, and I knew it was going to take some time for me to accept what I had done.

"What are they going to do with her body? How are you so sure nobody will find it?" I asked.

"They work for a coroner. They will take her there after hours and cremate her," Charlotte told me.

"Damn," I replied.

"That's how I knew Celly didn't kill Reggie. I wish she

would hide a body in her backyard with the pull I got. Soon as I find Kadarius, his ass will be in there next."

I laughed even though I knew she was serious. Sensing I was upset, Charlotte suggested the three of us go to her place and have some drinks. It was going to take a lot more than liquor to take my mind off of what happened, but it was a start. After this shit with Celeste's ex was over, we were all going on vacation, maybe even move. New York was starting to have too many bad memories.

Chapter 30: Pressure

It'd been two weeks since we disposed of Serenity's body, and I could tell it was still fucking with Devon's head. He took it hard the first night, and the best thing I could do was sit here and be his support system. I knew that Ren wasn't just a quick nut for him. She was his best friend, and I knew how it felt to lose a best friend. Sometimes I still thought about Jolani. Jolani was my ride or die, and I found myself dreaming about her sometimes. She was my girl, and there were days I still couldn't believe she was ripped away from me just like that. Sometimes I still blamed myself, and I hated it.

I didn't want that to happen to Devon. I didn't want him to get stuck into that dark place thinking that it was his fault. Part of me questioned if it was an accident, but I wouldn't question him because I didn't wanna put him through even more pain. He was slowly turning back to his old self, and I had myself to thank for that. I made it my mission to put a smile on his face every day. He went from not sleeping and eating to sleeping well and gaining weight like a fat bitch from *My 600-lb Life*. I love Devon, and his happiness mattered a lot to me.

I was so busy tending to my kids and making sure Devon was straight that I wasn't even aware of what was going on with myself. While Devon took the kids out to have fun, I decided to go for my usual checkup early. I guess I was so stressed out and busy, I didn't notice that my period was late. Finding out that I was pregnant had me baffled yet confused. I didn't know how to feel about this new life growing in my stomach. I felt like a hypocrite because I wasn't happy about my last pregnancy. However, the miscarriage hit me hard and to find out that I had another baby on the way gave me mixed emotions.

Devon was good with the kids, and we both had good careers, but was a baby what Devon wanted? I actually wanted to keep the baby, and I was praying that Devon was all for it. The thing was, how was I going to tell him? The more I thought about this baby growing inside of me, the wider my smile grew. Baby names were popping up in my head, and I even wanted to tell the kids that they had a sibling on the way. I just didn't wanna get too excited before I could come up with a final decision on what I wanted to do.

I was at the pharmacy with a grin as big as the sun picking up my prenatal vitamins. Once I got in my car, I put the keys in the ignition. My heart almost jumped out of my chest when I saw Kadarius in the rearview mirror, looking like one of those crazy ass people in those Lifetime movies. Before I could get out of the car, he pressed a knife to my side.

"Look, I don't wanna hurt you. All I wanna do is talk," he said frantically.

I was in such shock; I was scared to move or say anything that would trigger him to kill me and my unborn baby. I swallowed the huge lump in my throat before taking the keys out of the ignition.

"Kadarius, please —."

"I'm not gonna hurt you, I swear. I'll put the knife up if you promise me that you're not gonna run. Promise to talk to me."

"Kadarius."

"Promise me," he said barely above a whisper. Looking into the rearview, I locked eyes with him to see that his eyes were a tad bit red mixed with a yellow color. He looked horrible. His beard was growing wild, and his hair was so matted, you could break a comb going through it. Taking a deep breath, I decided to give him a chance to talk. He had a knife, and the last thing I wanted to do was put me and my child in danger. He was crazy enough to pin his ex-lover's murder on me, so I knew for a fact that he was crazy enough to kill me and leave me right in this parking lot.

"I promise," I sighed.

"I'm sorry."

"Okay. Is that all?"

"No, just listen. Promise you'll listen."

"I'm listening."

"I've been nothing but a dick to you, and you have had every right to do me the way you did. I cheated on you with Reggie and to this day, I regret it. I cry myself to sleep thinking of you and our family, baby. You're ahead of any other woman I've ever met, and I'm so glad that I met you."

"Where are you going with this?"

"You're too good for me, and I never deserved you in the first place. You're supportive, beautiful, and brilliant. You gave me two beautiful kids that I would die for, and I love you for that. I never knew how much I needed you until I lost you. Celly, I love you and I always will. You have been my rock since day one, and I was a fool to let you go. When Tykell did what he did, I should have been there for you. I wasn't there and I regret it, I really do. I'm supposed to be your husband, your man, your protector. I know none of this is gonna get us back together, but I've been wanting to get this off of my chest. Lately, I've been playing the victim, and I should have never done that knowing that you were the true victim of all this bullshit. If I would have never stepped out on our marriage, you and this whole Tykell shit may not have ever happened. I knew I lost you for good when I saw that new nigga all up on you. Not to even sound cocky, but he'll never be me. He'll never replace what we had. I may have been a bad husband from time to time, but we were a good pair."

"You got one thing right."

"What?"

"He'll never be you. He's better. He loves me, he trusts me, and most of all, he believes in me. Devon treats the kids like they're his own, and he treats me like you should have treated me — like a woman. You treated me like shit through it all. I don't want you to think I left you because you cheated on me. We could have fixed it if you cheated on me with a woman. But you cheated on me with a nigga. A man. There's no going back after that. You made me feel like complete shit, and I hate you for it. If you came here looking for validation, you wasted your time. I hate you, and I always will. You were supposed to be that person I confided in and gave my all to, but you weren't. I hate you, and I will never forgive you for what you put me through. See, Devon told me that forgiveness isn't for you, it's for me. But I'm not gonna sit here and lie to you and tell you that I forgive you when I don't. If that's all you have to say, you can leave."

"Thank you for that. Congratulations on the new baby, by the way," he replied, looking over at the prenatal vitamins.

"Thanks."

"I will always love you. Tell KJ and Cassie I love them too. I promise, this will be the last time you ever see me."

"Goodbye, Kadarius."

"Goodbye, Celly," he replied, twisting his wedding ring off and placing it in my hands before getting out of the car. I let out a deep breath before reaching for my phone and calling the police.

Chapter 31: When A Good Thing Goes Bad

I sat in the empty house that I created my family in. After everything that went down, Celeste decided to sell our home. Everything was gone — the furniture, the photos, and most importantly, the memories. All I could do was sit in the middle of the floor in the living room, staring at the tiny holes in the wall that once had nails to hold up our family picture. I laid back on the hardwood floors, looking up at the ceiling fan. Closing my eyes, memories faded into my mind like a polaroid.

"I put that shit on everything. I bet I can pull her," said my teammate, Harvey. We were wrapping things up after a long practice, and due to the coach's wife going into labor, we were excused from practice early. Since I knew for a fact that I didn't have anything else to do when I got home, Harvey and I sat out and watched the girls practice track.

"You not pulling shit. That girl shot you down how many times?" I laughed to myself, wiping the beads of sweat from my forehead.

"Celeste shoot every nigga down. Her head always in a got damn book."

"That's not even your type of girl anyway. You'd usually go for her sister. That damn Charlotte is something else."

"Man, who you tellin'? I'm not tryna fuck with Charlotte. That girl too wild for me."

"Nigga, you wild as hell yourself. How somebody too wild for you?"

"She just is," he laughed.

"Well, stop pursuing Celeste; she already spoken for."

"And who speaks for her fine ass? She's probably dating one of those punk ass nerds."

"Nah, I'm fuckin' with her."

"Quit fuckin' with me. You ain't fuckin' with that."

"I am."

"I call bullshit."

"We went on a date and everything. I'm cuffing that."

"Prove it. If I call her over and ask if y'all fuckin' —"

"I never said we were fuckin'. I said we were talking."

"Fucking, talking, same thing."

"And that's why your ass stays in trouble with these girls. Fucking and talking are not the same thing."

"Aight, I'm gonna chill. But how is she, though? She fine as hell, but she look like she'll bore a nigga to death."

"Don't worry about her. Just know I got that on lock."

"I won't believe it until I see it."

Before I could respond, Celeste was jogging over in her Nike shorts and sport bra with sweat dripping from every inch of her body. Her hair was pulled back into a ponytail, showing every ounce of her beauty.

"Hey." She smiled with her hands on her hips, trying to catch her breath.

"Wassup," I greeted, lighting up brighter than the blistering sun that hung over our heads.

"I thought you would have been gone by now since the coach let you guys leave early."

"Nah, I wanted to watch my girl."

"Watch me die in this heat."

"Just watch you in general. You know I love to see you beat all these other girls on this field."

"Mhm, well I just finished. My sister and my friends ditching me to go to get pizza. I swear they are gonna pizza me to death."

"What you wanna get?"

"I'm in the mood for chicken."

"You know that's what your name is saved as in my phone, right? You love you some damn chicken."

"I know you do not have me saved as Chicken in your phone," she laughed.

"I do, for real."

"Wow, my feelings are hurt."

"Get your stuff. Let's go get some. I can go for some chicken anyway."

"Really."

"Yeah, as long as you let me pay this time."

"I'll think about it." She blushed before running off to get her belongings.

"Well, ain't that some shit?" laughed Harvey watching Celeste's ass jiggle in her shorts.

"Keep your eyes in your head, nigga. Like I said, she's spoken for."

"What did you do to get that?"

"Shit, I'm still tryna bag her fully. She's something different, I'll tell you that."

"Different in a good way or bad way?"

"Just know she's different, and I like that shit." I smiled watching her jog back over to me.

"You better keep that one."

"You don't gotta tell me twice," I smirked.

"You ready to go, big head?" she grinned.

"That's if you ready to go, Chicken."

"Don't make me break up with you over that."

"Over calling you Chicken?"

"Yeah, that ain't cute."

"Whatever. Let's go, Chicken." I laughed watching her face turn red.

I laughed to myself at how whipped I was over Celeste in college. All I could do was laugh and reminisce on the good because I knew the bad would sooner rush in and take me under like a tsunami. Getting up off of the floor, I went into the bedroom I once shared with Celeste and looked around at the empty space.

"You fucked up. You know that, right?" said Reggie, once again fading into my mind.

"I had a feeling you would come back."

"Yeah, come back for you."

"You don't have to keep visiting me."

"Seems like I do."

"You don't because I got something that's gonna make it all go away."

"And what is that?"

I pulled the gun from the back of my pants before placing it at my head. I wanted this all to go away. I prayed to God, and my prayers went unanswered. I was feeling alone, and depression was sinking in like the Titanic. I swallowed the lump in my throat before looking around the room to see that Reggie was nowhere to be found.

"Do it," Reggie's voice said in my head.

"I will."

"Do it! Do it now!" his voice grew louder.

I clenched my eyes closed harder before asking God to forgive me for my sins. I placed my finger on the trigger, ready to blow my brains out.

RING, RING, RING

The sound of my phone interrupted me before I could do anything. Opening my eyes, I reached in my pocket to see Celeste's name flashing on my screen. Sliding my finger across the screen, I placed it on speaker before dropping to the floor and crying silently.

"Kadarius, did you break into our old house? I got a call from one of the neighbors saying your car is outside. You know they called the cops, right?"

"Just like you called the police that day. Don't act worried about me."

"I'm not worried about you because you're a grown ass man who needs to take responsibility for his actions."

"I'm gonna miss that."

"Miss what?"

"That bossy ass attitude of yours. Even though it got on my nerves sometimes, it sure as hell got me straight. Can you do me a favor?"

"I'm not doing anything for you."

"Did you tell the kids I loved them?"

"No, I didn't. You can tell them once you go to jail. I'm pretty sure they already know you love them, Kadarius."

"Are you around them?"

"Yeah, why?"

"Can I talk to Cassie?"

"Make it quick."

I heard shuffling in the background before Cassie's voice rang through the phone.

"Hello," she chirped.

"Hey, Princess, it's Daddy."

"Hey, Daddy."

"I missed you."

"I missed you too."

"Where's KJ?"

"He's sleeping."

"Okay well, you can tell him what I'm about to tell you."

"Okay."

"You know I love you, right?"

"Yeah."

"I love you, your brother, and your mama. I will always love the three of you, and I would do anything in the world for any of you."

"I love you too."

"I just wanna tell you I'm sorry, Princess."

"Sorry for what, Daddy?"

"For not being there for you, your brother, and your mother when you guys needed me. I'm sorry for everything, and I never meant to hurt you guys," I cried.

"Daddy, why are you crying?"

"Because I love you, baby girl. Tell KJ I love him too and I will always love him. I want you to do me a favor. Look after your brother and your mother for me, okay?"

"Why? Where are you going?"

"Daddy's gonna be gone for a few. This is gonna be the last

time we talk."

"Cassie, go check on your brother. Let me talk to your daddy," said Celeste, taking the phone. I heard shuffling before she began to talk.

"I'm assuming you're turning yourself in."

"I'm not. I'm actually happy you called. Celeste, I can't do this anymore."

"You can't do what?"

"I can't live with this guilt. I wanna make it all go away, Celeste," I cried.

"KD, you're not talking straight. What do you mean?"

I heard sirens blaring outside before an officer on the intercom called for me to come out with my hands up.

"Take care of my kids for me. I love you, Chicken," I simply replied, putting the phone on the floor. I ignored her calls for me to answer her. As soon as I heard the police kick the doors in downstairs, I placed the gun back at my head and took a deep breath.

"Kadarius, talk to me, please!" Celeste screamed in the phone.

"Forgive me," I said before pulling the trigger, ending all the pain and suffering, ending everything.

Epilogue

Celeste

Five Years Later

"One, Two, Three, Go!" On the count of three, we let our balloons cloud the sky as we stood in the yard. Devon and I decided on planning a get together to celebrate the lives of the people we lost. We tried to do this almost every year. Not only did we release a balloon for Jolani and Ren, but we released one for Kadarius as well. The day he killed himself, I couldn't do anything but break down and cry like a baby. Even though we were going through hell with one another, to hear him call me Chicken and pull the trigger, sent my heart on a rollercoaster ride. I couldn't believe he was really gone, and the sad part was that I missed him, I really missed him. The kids missed him more, and I knew that this balloon release would give them hope that their father was watching over them from Heaven. I knew that Kadarius was going straight to hell for everything he'd done, but I wanted the kids to think that he went to Heaven to make things better for them.

After five years, life had changed drastically for me, and in a good way. Despite me having to go to therapy after losing Kadarius and having a hard pregnancy due to stress, everything was going well for me. I gave birth to a healthy baby boy named Jevon, and I couldn't have been happier to have birthed that little human. He stole Devon's whole face and to this day, I was heated about that.

So much had gone on in New York, so Devon and I decided to pack up and move to Philly. It was different and it bettered both of our careers. I wrote a story on everything that had happened to me, and I was bringing in even more money than I could count. I was now a New York Times Best Seller, and I even had movie deals coming.

The life I was fighting so hard to get was finally sitting in the palm of my hands, and I loved it. At times, I still thought about Tykell and Kadarius. I thought about how damaged both men were and how I was that structure for them. I thought about how I was the reason both of them were dead. Sometimes I blamed myself for all of the bad that occurred in my life, but when I looked in the mirror and I saw Devon behind me, all that blame went out of the window. Devon was my rock and I, his. He showed me that I didn't have to be scared to let another man in, that I didn't have to always feel alone.

After everyone left, Devon and I were laid in bed, looking up at the mirror on the ceiling at three of the kids fast asleep in our California King bed. All three of them laid in between us. Regardless of how big Cassie and KJ were, they still acted as if they were babies, and I didn't mind it at all.

"Thank you," said Devon, tracing my wedding ring.

"For what?" I smiled.

"For being my peace."

"Thank you for being the shoulder I always needed."

"I'll always be here."

"I love you."

"I love you too."

"Show me how much," he smirked.

"Meet me in the bathroom downstairs." I smiled, climbed out of bed, and headed downstairs. He was right behind me. I couldn't even make it there by myself before he had me pinned up against the wall. I was convinced that he was trying to work on baby number four. This man was something else. He was mine.

The End

WANT TO INTERACT WITH T'ANN MARIE & HER TEAM? JOIN OUR READERS GROUP ON FACEBOOK @ *T'ANN MARIE PRESENTS: DOPE ASS READS!* WIN PRIZES, BE APART OF LIVE BOOK DISCUSSIONS & MORE!

Join Our Mailing List:

http://eepurl.com/gU81k5

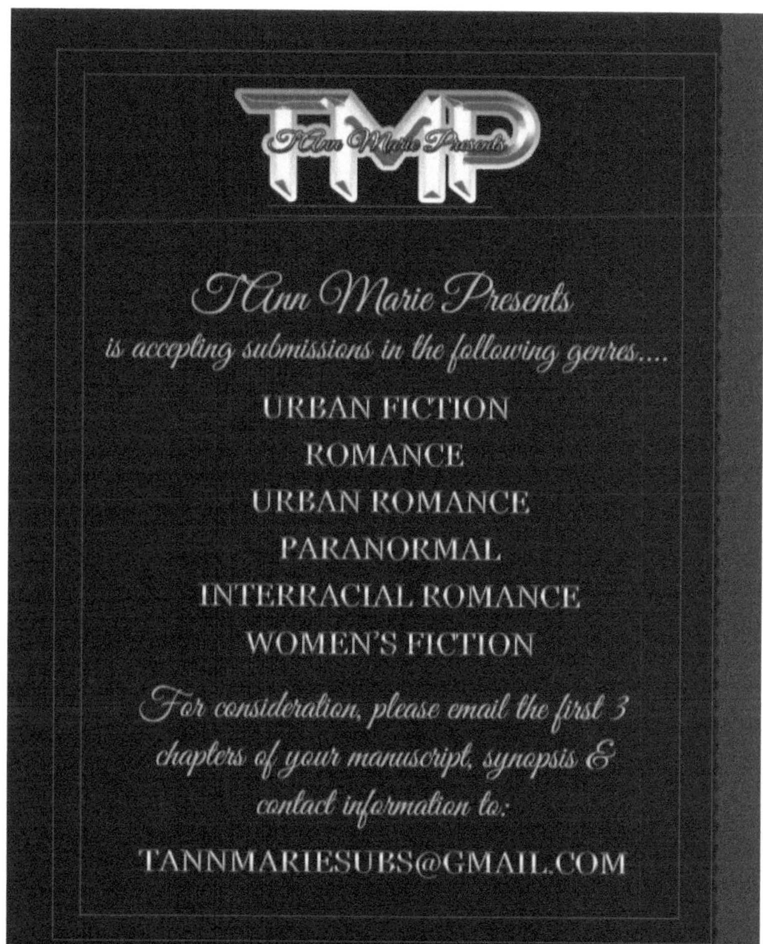
TAnn Marie Presents
is accepting submissions in the following genres....
URBAN FICTION
ROMANCE
URBAN ROMANCE
PARANORMAL
INTERRACIAL ROMANCE
WOMEN'S FICTION
For consideration, please email the first 3
chapters of your manuscript, synopsis &
contact information to:
TANNMARIESUBS@GMAIL.COM

www.ingramcontent.com/pod-product-compliance
Lightning Source LLC
Chambersburg PA
CBHW030309160726
47992CB00005B/1942